SHIPWRECKED ON MAD ISLAND

DAN JOLLEY

ILLUSTRATED BY

COURTNEY HUDDLESTON

GRAPHIC UNIVERSE™ · MINNEAPOLIS · NEW YORK

Story by Dan Jolley

Pencils and inks by Courtney Huddleston

Coloring by Hi-Fi Design

Lettering by Marshall Dillon

Copyright © 2009 by Lerner Publishing Group, Inc.

Graphic Universe™ is a trademark and Twisted Journeys® is a registered trademark of Lerner Publishing Group, Inc.

Graphic Universe
A division of Lerner Publishing Group, Inc.
241 First Avenue North
Minneapolis, MN 55401 U.S.A.

Website address: www.lernerbooks.com

Library of Congress Cataloging-in-Publication Data

Jolley, Dan.
　　Shipwrecked on Mad Island / story by Dan Jolley ; pencils and inks by Courtney Huddleston.
　　　　p.　　cm. —— (Twisted journeys)
　　Summary: As the hero of this graphic novel who is shipwrecked and stranded on an island during a school field trip, the reader is asked to make choices throughout the story to avoid being harmed by strange, half-human creatures.
　　　ISBN: 978-0-8225-7911-3 (lib. bdg. : alk. paper)
　　　1. Plot-your-own stories. 2. Graphic novels. [1. Graphic novels. 2. Castaways—Fiction. 3. Shipwrecks—Fiction. 4. Animal experimentation—Fiction. 5. Science fiction. 6. Plot-your-own stories.] I. Huddleston, Courtney, ill. II. Title.
PZ7.7.J65Shi 2009
741.5'973—dc22　　　　　　　　　　　　　　　　　　　　　　　　2008026735

Manufactured in the United States of America
1 2 3 4 5 6 – DP – 14 13 12 11 10 09

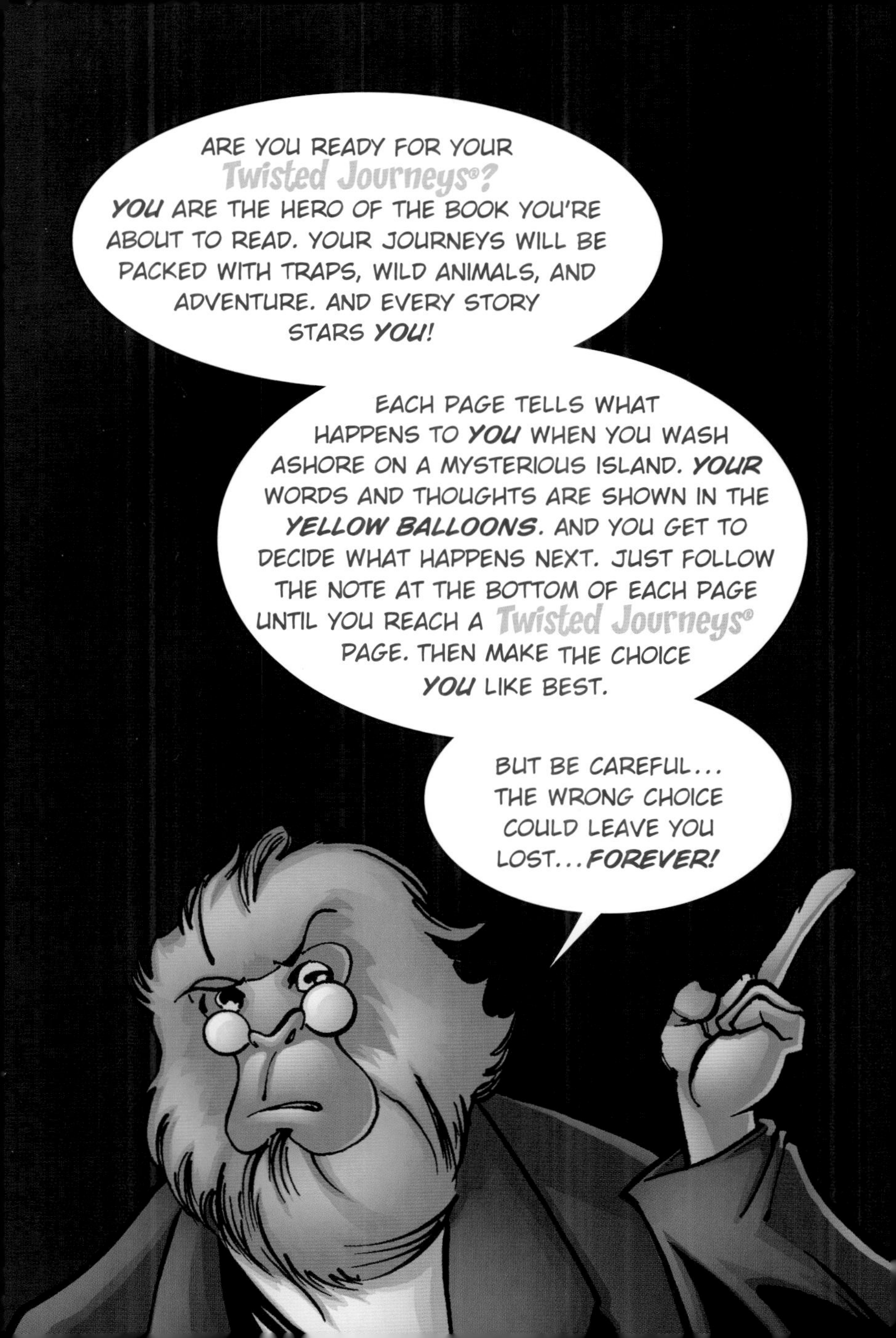
ARE YOU READY FOR YOUR Twisted Journeys®? YOU ARE THE HERO OF THE BOOK YOU'RE ABOUT TO READ. YOUR JOURNEYS WILL BE PACKED WITH TRAPS, WILD ANIMALS, AND ADVENTURE. AND EVERY STORY STARS YOU!
EACH PAGE TELLS WHAT HAPPENS TO YOU WHEN YOU WASH ASHORE ON A MYSTERIOUS ISLAND. YOUR WORDS AND THOUGHTS ARE SHOWN IN THE YELLOW BALLOONS. AND YOU GET TO DECIDE WHAT HAPPENS NEXT. JUST FOLLOW THE NOTE AT THE BOTTOM OF EACH PAGE UNTIL YOU REACH A Twisted Journeys® PAGE. THEN MAKE THE CHOICE YOU LIKE BEST.
BUT BE CAREFUL... THE WRONG CHOICE COULD LEAVE YOU LOST...FOREVER!

The salty ocean water engulfs you as you plunge in headfirst.

It's dark under the waves, and you hear the distorted voices of your classmates calling your name. The oblong shape of the lifeboat rapidly grows smaller as another gigantic wave crashes into it and pushes it farther away from you. Your friends lean over the edge, stretching their arms out to you, but they can't reach you.

This was supposed to be a fun, peaceful field trip for biology class. You never expected a huge storm to come up . . . and you *really* never expected the ship you were on to hit a reef . . . and you *really, really* never expected to get thrown out of the lifeboat!

But here you are. You gasp as you break the surface and stare after the retreating boat.

You know you'll never catch it.

GO ON TO THE NEXT PAGE.

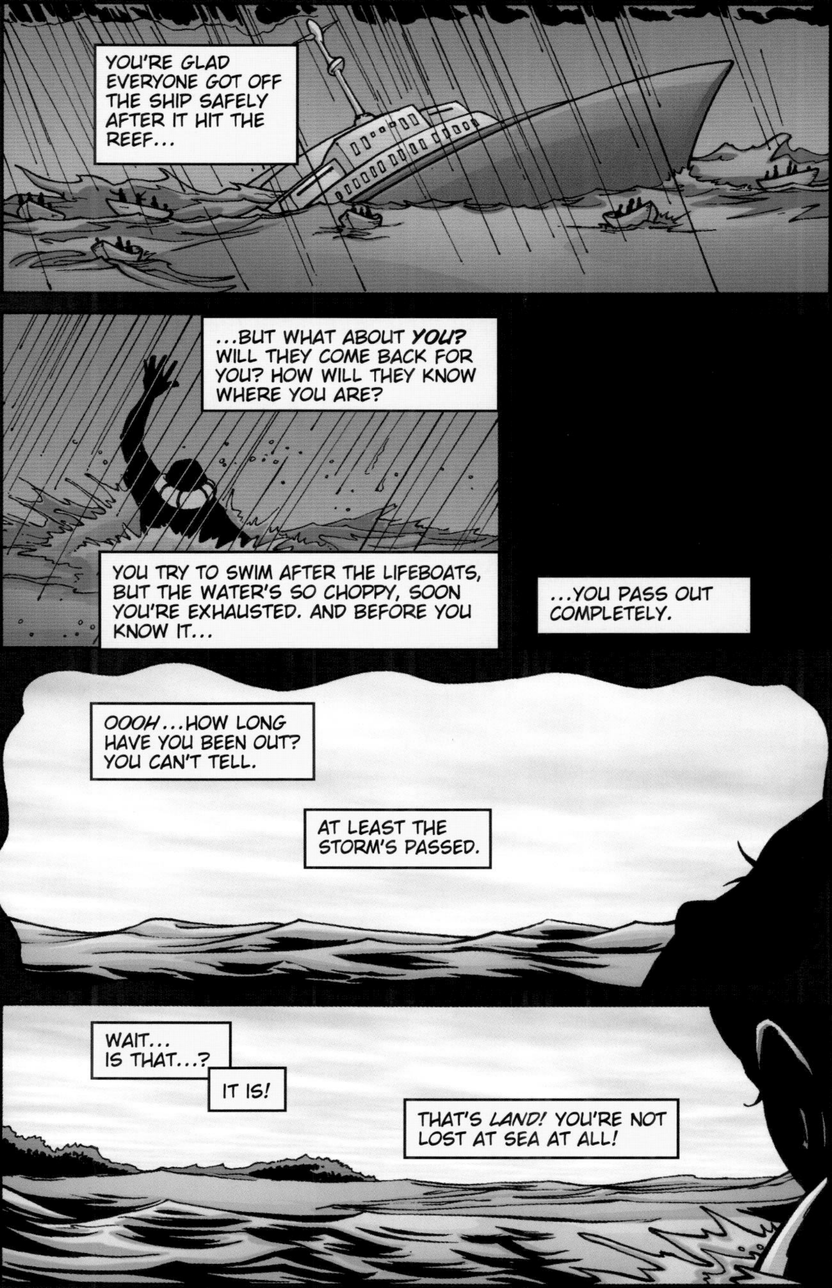
YOU'RE GLAD EVERYONE GOT OFF THE SHIP SAFELY AFTER IT HIT THE REEF...
...BUT WHAT ABOUT *YOU?* WILL THEY COME BACK FOR YOU? HOW WILL THEY KNOW WHERE YOU ARE?
YOU TRY TO SWIM AFTER THE LIFEBOATS, BUT THE WATER'S SO CHOPPY, SOON YOU'RE EXHAUSTED. AND BEFORE YOU KNOW IT...
...YOU PASS OUT COMPLETELY.
OOOH...HOW LONG HAVE YOU BEEN OUT? YOU CAN'T TELL.
AT LEAST THE STORM'S PASSED.
WAIT... IS THAT...?
IT IS!
THAT'S *LAND!* YOU'RE NOT LOST AT SEA AT ALL!

GO ON TO THE NEXT PAGE.

The thin dark line of the distant shore seems to be miles and miles away, though.

The orange life jacket strapped around your body saved your life. You have no doubts about that. But it makes it awfully difficult to swim well.

Nevertheless, you start moving toward the island. It's slow going. Soon you're tired. Soon after that, you're exhausted. But maybe your luck isn't all bad. You realize the waves are carrying you straight toward the shoreline.

Eventually the ocean washes you up onto the beach like a piece of driftwood. You stretch out on the sand and listen to the calls of unfamiliar birds. Dense jungle begins where the beach ends.

You just lie there for a while, grateful to be on land, and let your strength come back.

It's then that you see the dark, angry storm clouds over the water— heading your way.

GO ON TO THE NEXT PAGE.

TWISTED JOURNEYS®

That storm will be on top of you in minutes!

WILL YOU . . .

. . . stay near the beach and try to find some shelter here?

TURN TO PAGE 16.

. . . head into the island's jungle interior?

TURN TO PAGE 30.

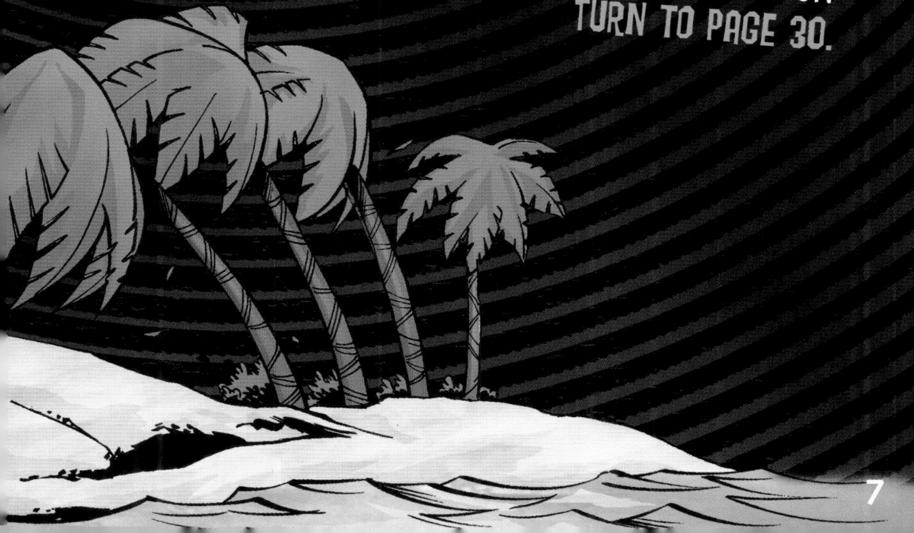

This bird is *huge*! If it decides to eat you, you'll be a bite-size meal for it!

WILL YOU . . .

. . . hang onto its feet for dear life, since you're so high up?
TURN TO PAGE 12.

. . . try to break free of its hold when you pass over one of the lakes you saw?
TURN TO PAGE 60.

Slowly, quietly, you start down the hallway.

Immediately, you see what smelled so bad: large piles of . . . well, it's poop of some kind. You're not sure what kind of animal would have made that, but the mess is big enough that you're not anxious to find out. Ahead of you, at the end of the hall, you see a large metal door.

Slowly . . . carefully . . . foot by foot, you pad toward the door . . . and it's unlocked! You open it and slip inside . . .

. . . into a room lined with bookshelves. You barricade the door, then you see a *radio* on a table in the center of the floor!

Seconds later, static from the radio fills the room then focuses into a voice: "This is the U.S. Coast Guard. Who's using this channel?"

"Someone with a story you'll never believe in a million years," you say into the microphone, your voice thick with relief. "Come get me, and I'll tell you all about it."

THE END

THESE PEOPLE ARE SO SINCERE... AND THEY *REALLY* NEED YOUR HELP. HOW COULD YOU REFUSE?

YOU HAVE NO IDEA WHO YOU'RE GOING TO TALK TO, BUT SURELY YOU CAN THINK OF *SOMEONE*.

WE SALVAGED THIS BOAT WHEN IT WASHED UP ONSHORE ONE DAY.

IT WILL GET YOU TO THE MAINLAND.

ONE OF THE HALF HUMANS USED TO BE A SHIP'S CAPTAIN. HE EXPLAINS ALL THE DETAILS YOU NEED TO KNOW ABOUT OPERATING THE BOAT.

YOU SHAKE HANDS WITH EVERYONE AND START THE LITTLE ENGINE.

10

GO ON TO THE NEXT PAGE.

It takes a couple of days. Several times, you think for sure you're hopelessly lost at sea, but you finally do make it to the mainland. The first thing you do is look up animal rights activists . . . then you look up human rights activists . . . and you're not sure which is more appropriate, so you talk to both groups.

Next, you alert the military. You would go to the police, but you're pretty sure they're not equipped to deal with a bizarre problem on an island in the middle of the ocean. With the military, you might have better luck.

You end up talking to a Colonel Robert Croy. You're intensely relieved that he takes you seriously. "This is something we have to fix," he says, clapping his hat onto his head. "Come on, kid. Let's go fix it."

TURN TO PAGE 66.

The bird is enormous and terrifying, but it also has you dangling about eight hundred feet in the air. You decide you won't be breaking loose.

Soon the bird begins to descend, and you see something below, nestled in among the treetops. The closer you get, the clearer it becomes. You're looking at a *house*, made almost entirely of bamboo, built into the top of one of the jungle's biggest trees.

This isn't a tree house you'd expect someone to build in a backyard, either. As the bird drops lower, you see that the house has three different levels, with really neat angles and lots of windows.

The bird takes you to a large, open balcony, sets you down very gently, and flies away.

GO ON TO THE NEXT PAGE.

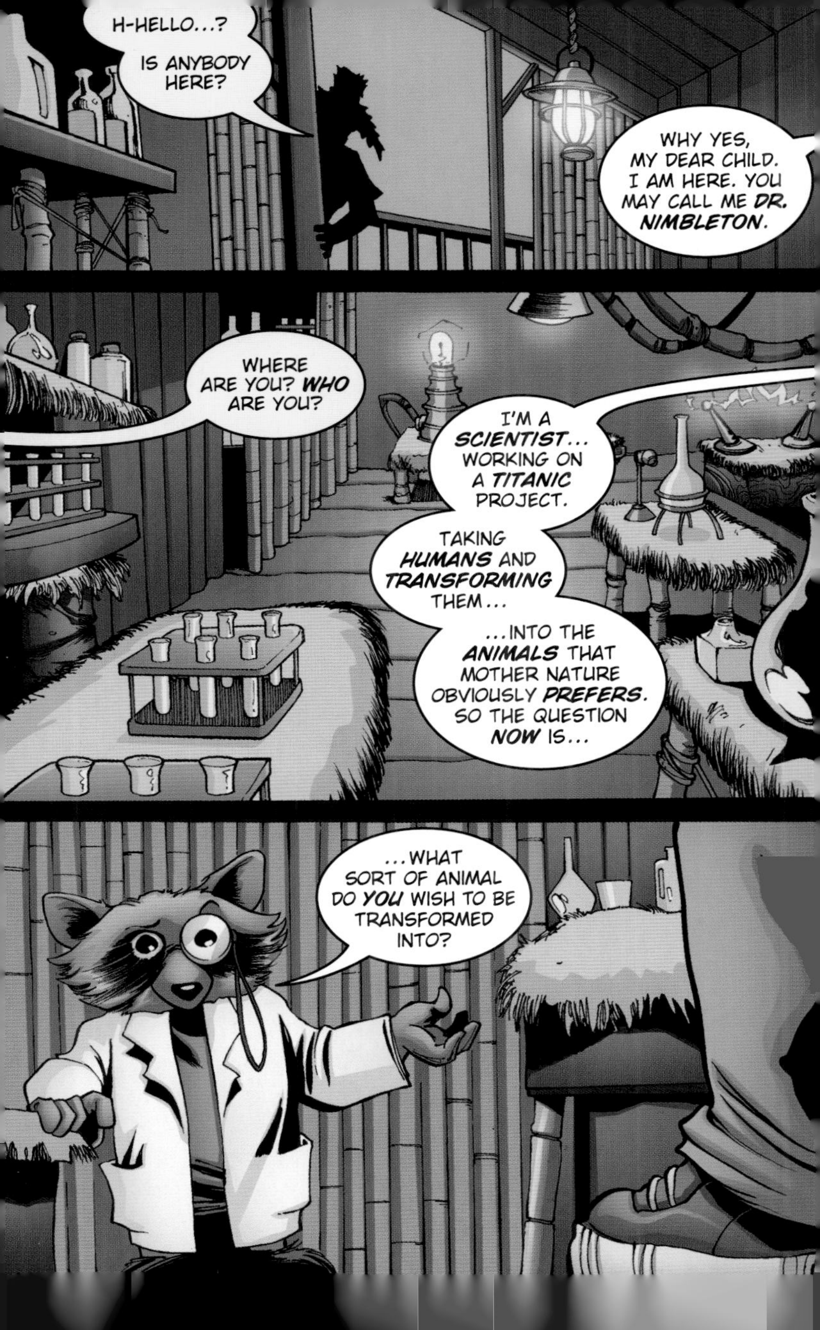
H-HELLO...?
IS ANYBODY HERE?
WHY YES, MY DEAR CHILD. I AM HERE. YOU MAY CALL ME DR. NIMBLETON.
WHERE ARE YOU? WHO ARE YOU?
I'M A SCIENTIST... WORKING ON A TITANIC PROJECT.
TAKING HUMANS AND TRANSFORMING THEM...
...INTO THE ANIMALS THAT MOTHER NATURE OBVIOUSLY PREFERS. SO THE QUESTION NOW IS...
...WHAT SORT OF ANIMAL DO YOU WISH TO BE TRANSFORMED INTO?

This is *crazy*. You're talking to a raccoon, for crying out loud! And you're not about to let him turn you into some sort of animal, either!

WILL YOU . . .

. . . tell Nimbleton that you DO NOT want to be turned into an animal?
TURN TO PAGE 45.

. . . forget trying to reason with this creature and run as fast as your legs will take you?
TURN TO PAGE 27.

You remember reading somewhere that in case of a tornado, if you're caught outdoors with no shelter, you should get into the lowest part of the land you can find, like a ditch or a hole. Well, there are plenty of holes around here, what with all the trees getting uprooted.

You dive into a hole and huddle at the bottom. It's barely big enough to hold you, but you make yourself as flat as possible.

Then the immense force of the wind grabs hold of your body and starts pulling. It's not working! The hole's too shallow! You scream and try to hold on . . .

. . . but you're lifted into the air, right up into the hurricane.

You have a few seconds to regret your decision. Then you see a palm tree coming straight for you at about a hundred miles an hour. And that's . . .

THE END

You're not sure what you might encounter if you go too deep into that jungle. Plus, the trees at the beach's edge are tall and densely packed. You bet you could find a good place to wait out the storm right here.

Carefully, you step just into the edge of the jungle. A plant with long, broad leaves grows nearby, and you pull one of them off. With a little work, you turn it into a hat. It's not an umbrella, no, but it should help keep the rain off your head.

Almost immediately, dense sheets of rain start smashing down. This storm could be a hurricane! There's a hollow at the base of a huge tree . . . you could take shelter there . . .

. . . but then you think you see a tiny spot of *light*, somewhere deep in the jungle.

GO ON TO THE NEXT PAGE.

The storm gets more vicious by the
second. You're afraid it's going to turn
into a full-blown hurricane!

WILL YOU . . .

. . . dig deeper into the
shelter you found at the
base of the tree?
TURN TO PAGE 42.

. . . run into the jungle
and try to find that light?
TURN TO PAGE 74.

It's time to throw caution to the wind! You scoot along the ledge as fast as you can, determined to make it to the wide shelf in as little time as possible.

And it might have worked, if you hadn't stepped on one particularly loose rock. The ledge gives way, and as you fall—

—passing the rest of the shelf, where you see an entire campsite set up, with tents and a campfire and surprised-looking campers sitting there staring at you with wide eyes—

—you find yourself thinking, *maybe I should've been more careful.*

But there's no more time for regret, as the rocks at the base of the cliff come rushing toward you really, *really* quickly.

THE END

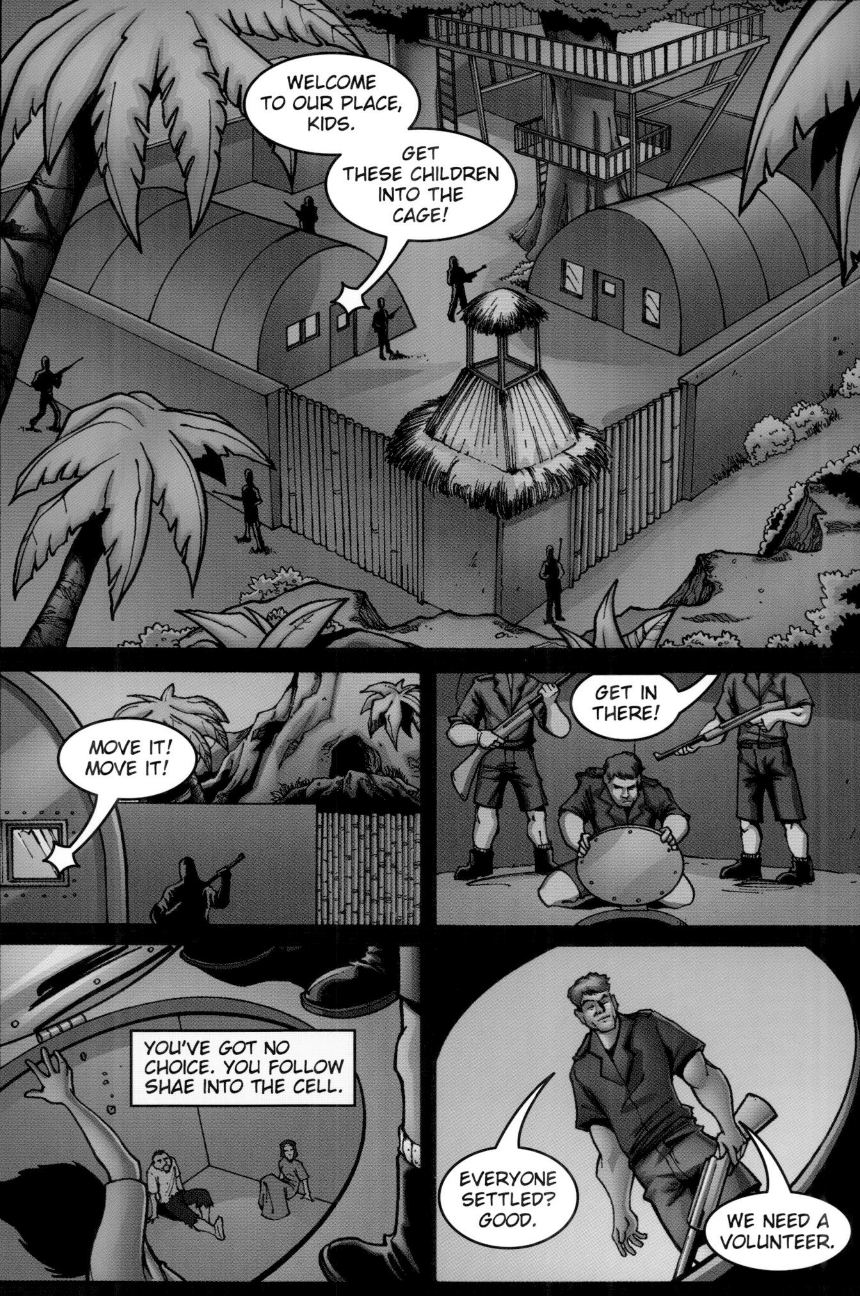
WELCOME TO OUR PLACE, KIDS.
GET THESE CHILDREN INTO THE CAGE!
MOVE IT! MOVE IT!
GET IN THERE!
YOU'VE GOT NO CHOICE. YOU FOLLOW SHAE INTO THE CELL.
EVERYONE SETTLED? GOOD.
WE NEED A VOLUNTEER.

GO ON TO THE NEXT PAGE.

You're pretty sure these guys are evil.
They might even be crazy! Who knows
what you'd be volunteering for?

WILL YOU . . .

. . . keep quiet and stay put in the cage?

TURN TO PAGE 26.

. . . raise your hand and speak up?

TURN TO PAGE 54.

You didn't have to worry, as it turns out. As soon as the half-crocodile thugs start to move in, Mongoose explodes up off the floor and turns into a tornado of fists, feet, knees, and elbows. In seconds, all of Dr. Nimbleton's men—or half men—lie unconscious on the floor.

Nimbleton's not so tough now. "There's no need to use violence!" he says as Mongoose walks over to him. "I'll come quietly! I won't resist!"

Mongoose comes to you after tying up Dr. Nimbleton. "Okay, *now* we'll get you to safety, so you can go back home."

"Sorry I didn't help out more," you say quietly.

Mongoose shrugs. "It's not your job, y'know? Your job is to go home and lead a normal life. Leave all this craziness to people qualified to handle it."

You know Mongoose is right. But as you're leaving the island in an unmarked helicopter, your "normal life" seems so . . . *normal!*

THE END

There's no cover anywhere around you. The best thing you could hope for is to make a run for it . . . and so that's exactly what you do. Even though your legs still hurt like crazy from the drop into the lake, you make them move—and move *fast*.

The half humans weren't expecting you to run, and you get all the way to the tree line before they catch up with you. Of course, when they do catch up with you, you feel kind of stupid for trying to get away from them on foot. They're all at least twice as fast as you are. A couple of them literally start running circles around you.

But something occurs to you: *They're not hurting you.* They don't even look as if they *want* to hurt you. They're all just sort of swarming around.

You come to a stop and clear your throat.

GO ON TO THE NEXT PAGE.

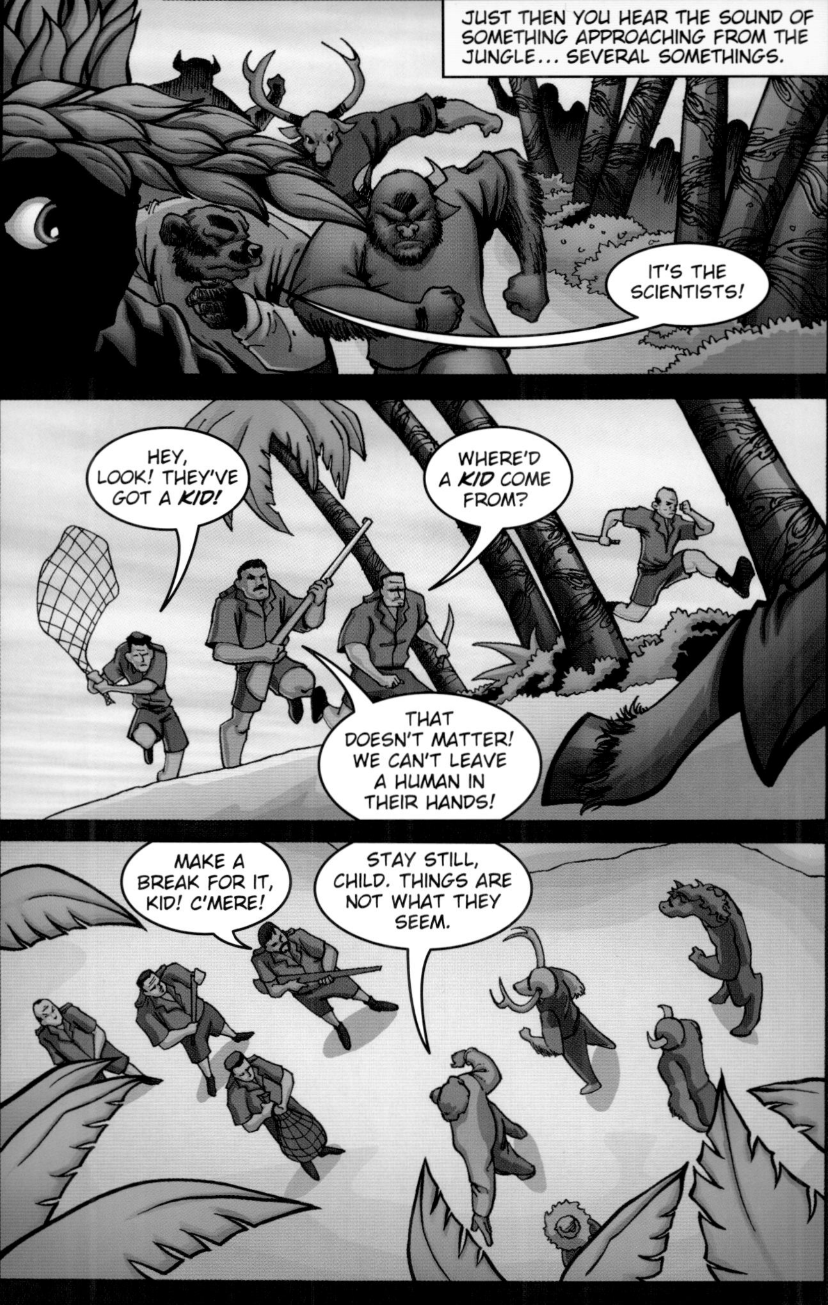
JUST THEN YOU HEAR THE SOUND OF SOMETHING APPROACHING FROM THE JUNGLE... SEVERAL SOMETHINGS.
IT'S THE SCIENTISTS!
HEY, LOOK! THEY'VE GOT A ***KID!***
WHERE'D A ***KID*** COME FROM?
THAT DOESN'T MATTER! WE CAN'T LEAVE A HUMAN IN THEIR HANDS!
MAKE A BREAK FOR IT, KID! C'MERE!
STAY STILL, CHILD. THINGS ARE NOT WHAT THEY SEEM.

GO ON TO THE NEXT PAGE.

You're completely weirded out by these bizarre creatures . . . but they seem peaceful. The scientists, on the other hand, are kind of scary . . . but they're human.

WILL YOU . . .

. . . trust the scientists and run to them?
TURN TO PAGE 105.

. . . stick with the half humans?
TURN TO PAGE 33.

You make your way around the rock face, picking your way over some loose boulders, until you see a path leading up the side of the mountain. Grateful that you didn't have to climb the wall, you set off up the path, looking forward to reaching the summit.

Finally, you come around a bend in the path . . . and there it is. The rest of the island, there for your examination.

But then you hear that strange squeaking again. And it's much louder now.

Turning your head, you see that you're standing in front of a huge, dark cave right up at the mountain's crest. And from within the cave . . . was that movement?

That's all the time you have for thinking, as suddenly hundreds upon hundreds of bloodthirsty *giant bats* pour out of the cave and swarm all over you, their fangs huge and sharp and glistening.

THE END

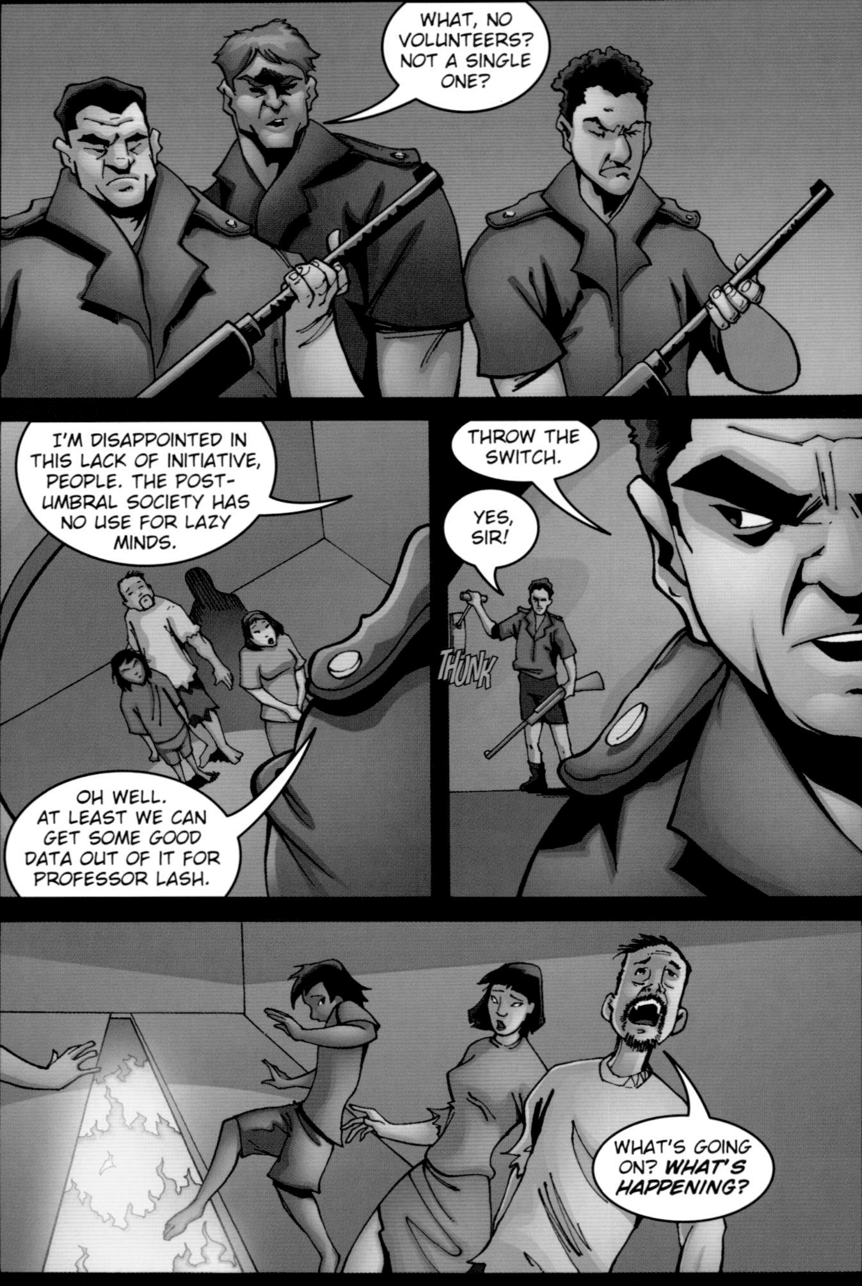
WHAT, NO VOLUNTEERS? NOT A SINGLE ONE?
I'M DISAPPOINTED IN THIS LACK OF INITIATIVE, PEOPLE. THE POST-UMBRAL SOCIETY HAS NO USE FOR LAZY MINDS.
OH WELL. AT LEAST WE CAN GET SOME GOOD DATA OUT OF IT FOR PROFESSOR LASH.
THROW THE SWITCH.
YES, SIR!
THUNK
WHAT'S GOING ON? ***WHAT'S HAPPENING?***

TURN TO PAGE 41.

You dash out onto the balcony where the bird dropped you off, but there's nowhere to go from there but down. And it's a *long* way down. But then suddenly a hand reaches down and grabs the back of your shirt . . .

. . . and hauls you right off your feet and up to the roof! Your rescuer is a young person dressed all in black, wearing a full-face black mask with high-tech goggles. *Is that a boy or a girl?* you wonder.

"No time for big explanations!" the masked stranger says. "Just three things you need to know. One: I'm Code name: Mongoose, secret agent, and I'm here to take down the evil geniuses on this island. That raccoon guy is one of them. Two: I know you're a civilian and I want to get you out of here and someplace safe, so follow my lead."

GO ON TO THE NEXT PAGE.

"Is there a three?" you ask after a moment.

"Yeah. Three: we've only got about a minute before Nimbleton sends some of his half-human thugs to try and kill us. So we've got to move fast!"

But it turns out you don't even have that long. There's a terrible cracking noise below your feet, and the whole section of roof you're standing on collapses.

You find yourself on the floor of Nimbleton's lab—and now you're surrounded by at least ten enormous creatures that look like crosses between humans and crocodiles.

The crash has destroyed a lot of Nimbleton's chemistry setup. You notice a bottle, still intact, on the floor near your foot. It has a big label on it: DANGER! DO NOT INHALE!

"I don't think I've ever seen two *less effective* young people," Nimbleton says. "Seeking glory, are we? You stop Dr. Nimbleton and you become international heroes?"

Mongoose groans in pain.

GO ON TO THE NEXT PAGE.

You're surrounded, and Mongoose might be badly hurt! But those half-crocodile guys look awfully fierce.

WILL YOU . . .

. . . keep quiet and still, and hope Mongoose can take care of the situation?

TURN TO PAGE 21.

. . . throw the bottle of chemicals at the bad guys?

TURN TO PAGE 39.

You know it won't do you any good to stay on the beach. Too much damage gets done to beaches during bad storms like this. So you head into the jungle, away from the water, toward the interior of the island.

It's not long before two things happen. First, the rain and wind slacken off, so much so that you're pretty sure they'll soon stop completely. Second . . . and weirder . . . the vegetation around you starts to look sort of odd. You've never been stranded on a jungle-covered desert island before, but still—these plants just plain don't look right.

You push through a dense bunch of leaves and discover a sort of pathway worn through the undergrowth. *Paths mean people!* You get so excited that you're practically running along the narrow dirt track.

Then you remember animals can make paths like this too . . . and that's when you hear the weird grunting and snuffling from just ahead of you.

GO ON TO THE NEXT PAGE.

AT FIRST YOU THINK YOU'RE HALLUCINATING.

BUT NO HALLUCINATION COULD *SMELL* THIS BAD.

STANDING THERE IN THE CLEARING IN FRONT OF YOU, BIG AS LIFE...

...IS A PREHISTORIC *GIANT GROUND SLOTH.*

YOU CAN'T REMEMBER FOR SURE HOW MANY TENS OF THOUSANDS OF YEARS AGO THESE THINGS WENT *EXTINCT...*

...BUT YOU KNOW IT WAS A *LOT.*

GO ON TO THE NEXT PAGE.

31

This is impossible!
That creature shouldn't even *exist!*

WILL YOU . . .

. . . run screaming from this
giant prehistoric beast?
TURN TO PAGE 63.

. . . steel your nerves and try to
make friends with it?
TURN TO PAGE 106.

Suddenly one of the scientists pulls a gun and starts firing at you!

"Take cover!" a wolf-woman shouts, pushing you to safety. The half humans pick up sticks, rocks, and even fallen coconuts and hurl them at the scientists. Soon the humans give up and retreat.

The wolf-woman and the bear-man come back to you. They explain that they used to be humans and were transformed by the scientists into the creatures you see before you. The scientists have been experimenting on shipwreck victims here for years.

You thank them for saving you. "How do I leave the island?" you ask.

They shake their heads. "No one leaves the island. I'm afraid you're stuck here. But we make a society the best we can here."

So . . . is that it? Is this your life now? Stuck on an island with a bunch of monsters, hunted by men with guns?

It sure looks that way.

THE END

SOMEHOW, WHEN YOU SUGGESTED DOING A NUMBER ON THE SCIENTISTS' EQUIPMENT, YOU DIDN'T EXPECT TO BE THE ONE WHO ACTUALLY CARRIED IT OUT.

AND YET HERE YOU ARE, IN A DISGUISE THE BEAR-MAN PUT TOGETHER, SNEAKING INTO THE PLACE.

THANK GOODNESS THE SCIENTISTS ARE ALL SO DISTRACTED WITH THEIR OWN RESEARCH.

THIS LOOKS LIKE THE PLACE.

PUSH A COUPLE OF BUTTONS, AND...

...*THERE* WE GO. THAT OUGHT TO HAVE AN EFFECT.

TRACKING CHIPS DEACTIVATED

GO ON TO THE NEXT PAGE.

As soon as you're back outside, you hear an ear-splitting chorus of war whoops. The half humans come pouring out of the jungle, dozens upon dozens of them. They storm their way into the base like an invading army. A really *loud* invading army.

You wander in after them and watch as half humans chase screaming scientists all over the place. The half humans poke the scientists with sticks . . . whap them across their heads . . . anything to get them to go to one spot: the huge cage in the center of the base.

You're pretty sure the scientists used to keep large game in this cage . . . or maybe some half humans. Today it holds nothing but guys in white coats.

The half humans ring around the scientists, some whooping, some laughing, some squawking.

TURN TO PAGE 82.

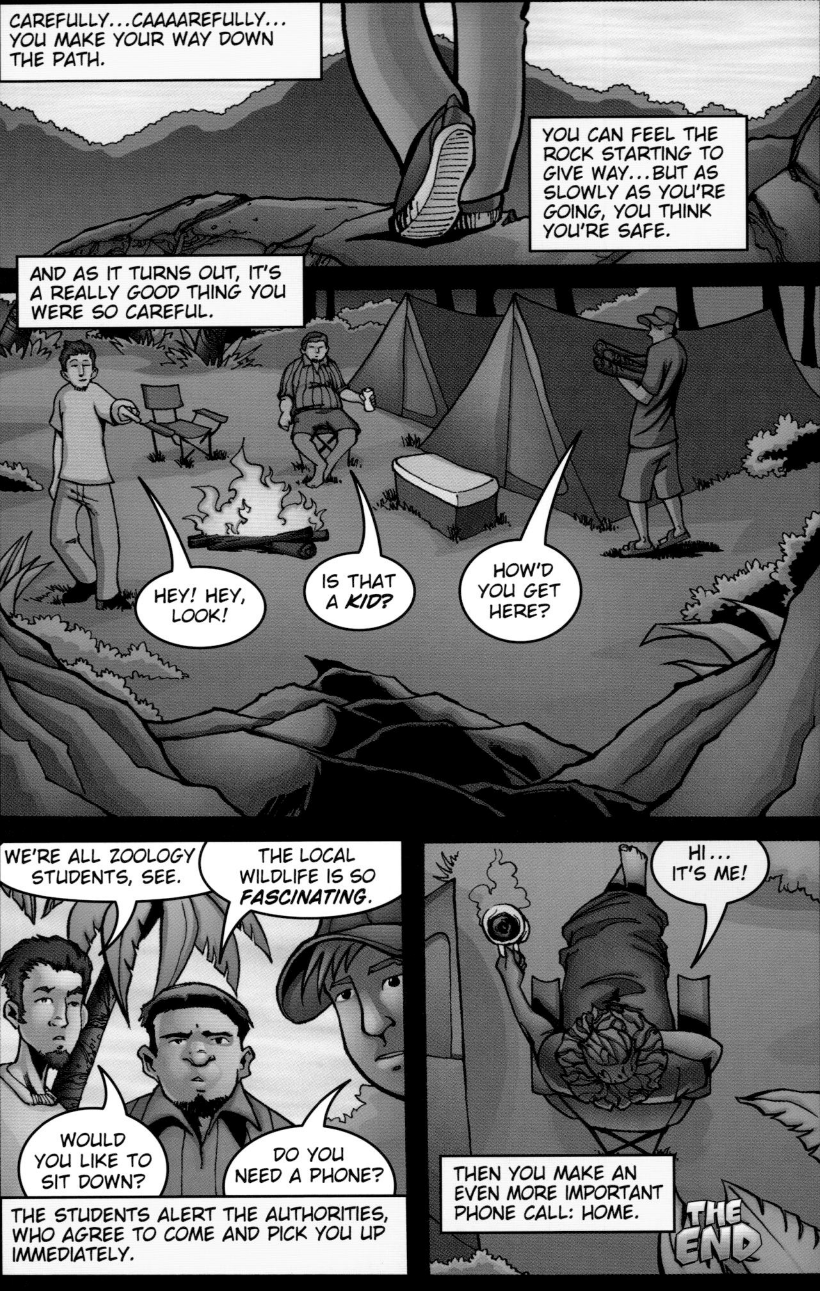
CAREFULLY...CAAAAREFULLY... YOU MAKE YOUR WAY DOWN THE PATH.
YOU CAN FEEL THE ROCK STARTING TO GIVE WAY...BUT AS SLOWLY AS YOU'RE GOING, YOU THINK YOU'RE SAFE.
AND AS IT TURNS OUT, IT'S A REALLY GOOD THING YOU WERE SO CAREFUL.
HEY! HEY, LOOK!
IS THAT A *KID?*
HOW'D YOU GET HERE?
WE'RE ALL ZOOLOGY STUDENTS, SEE.
THE LOCAL WILDLIFE IS SO *FASCINATING*.
WOULD YOU LIKE TO SIT DOWN?
DO YOU NEED A PHONE?
THE STUDENTS ALERT THE AUTHORITIES, WHO AGREE TO COME AND PICK YOU UP IMMEDIATELY.
HI... IT'S ME!
THEN YOU MAKE AN EVEN MORE IMPORTANT PHONE CALL: HOME.
THE END

Your arms feel like jelly, your lungs are burning, and you could swear your legs are about to fall off, but finally, you make it to the top of the sheer rock face. You hook one hand over the edge, dig your toe into a tiny crack, and with a last titanic effort of will, you heave yourself up.

You just lie there for a few seconds, too tired to move. But then your heart almost leaps straight out of your chest as you hear the sound of people talking!

A second wind lets you spring to your feet, and you see a narrow path running up through a crack in a gigantic rock. There *are* people up there! You can hear them! It sounds like there's a whole campsite, in fact.

You can't make out words yet. Maybe if you got a little closer . . . ?

GO ON TO THE NEXT PAGE.

Maybe these people could rescue you! But how do you know if they're friendly?

WILL YOU . . .

. . . run up and introduce yourself?
TURN TO PAGE 50.

. . . creep up the path a short distance so you can listen to them talking?
TURN TO PAGE 89.

You can't just lie there. You have to act!

In a flash, you reach down and grab the chemical bottle. You throw it as hard as you can at the floor right at Dr. Nimbleton's feet. The glass breaks, and a huge cloud of noxious-looking gas billows out of it.

Suddenly Mongoose is beside you, putting a filter mask over your nose and mouth, as Nimbleton and the half crocodiles all collapse to the floor, unconscious. "Thank you," the secret agent whispers. "I broke my leg in the fall. If you hadn't done that, we'd be goners."

Mongoose is impressed with you—impressed enough to see to it that word of what you did gets back to the top brass in the spy agency. Before you know it, you're being honored with a special secret-agent spy medal . . . and better yet, you get an offer to join the agency! You could work alongside Mongoose!

"Maybe," you tell them. "Maybe after junior high."

THE END

WILL YOU . . .

. . . agree to go for help,
if they have a way off the island?
TURN TO PAGE 10.

. . . refuse to help them in any way?
TURN TO PAGE 78.

. . . suggest sabotaging the
scientists' base of operations?
TURN TO PAGE 34.

The trapdoor in the bottom of the cage opens slowly but steadily. You look around at Shae and the other two captives. "What is this?" you ask the woman. "Do you know what's down there?"

She shakes her head, frightened. "I've never seen this before!"

You feel the heat even before you see the flickering light of the flames below. They're about to drop you into an incinerator!

"Are you recording all this?" the big man asks another hunter.

"Yes, sir!" the hunter answers. "I've got full documentation of the prisoners' reactions to extreme stress levels."

"Very good," the big man says. "Professor Lash can use that data in his next anthropological report."

As you fall, plummeting straight toward the deadly flames, you find yourself wishing that you'd stayed on the beach.

THE END

You press yourself into the hollow and try to fold up as tightly as you can, your back against one of the tree's big roots. With your arms wrapped around your knees and your face lowered, you hear the wind get louder . . . and louder . . . and *louder!*

The trees around you bend back and forth with the force of the wind. The rain comes at you sideways and stings your face, and to your horror, the tree you're hiding behind starts to come loose from the ground.

Then a tree to your right gets ripped completely up by its roots and spins away into the terrible, savage winds. You've got to move! You get to your feet and stumble farther into the jungle, half blind from the rain.

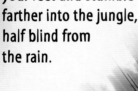

GO ON TO THE NEXT PAGE.

ANY SECOND NOW, THE STORM WILL BLOW YOU RIGHT OFF YOUR FEET!

YOU KNOW THE EYE OF A HURRICANE--THE CALM CENTER OF THE STORM-- IS A SAFE PLACE...

...BUT THE WINDS SURROUNDING IT TRAVEL AT HUNDREDS OF MILES AN HOUR.

IF YOU DON'T DO SOMETHING AND DO IT *SOON*, YOU'RE AS GOOD AS DEAD.

...IS THAT A *CAVE* UP THERE?

GO ON TO THE NEXT PAGE.

You've got to do something *now* or the hurricane will hit you the same way it's hitting those trees!

WILL YOU . . .

. . . turn around and head back to the beach, so you can try to get into the calm eye of the storm?

TURN TO PAGE 65.

. . . dive into one of the holes left by the uprooted trees, so the storm can pass over you?

TURN TO PAGE 15.

. . . head into the jungle after all and take shelter in the cave?

TURN TO PAGE 90.

"Um, I don't mean to be rude," you tell the raccoon, "but I don't want to be an animal."

Dr. Nimbleton blinks at you. "Really? Are you sure?"

"Yes, I'm sure! I'm a human! I want to *stay* a human."

The raccoon seems truly disappointed. "Oh, well, if that's the case . . ." His voice trails off—and suddenly his eyes gleam with a terrible light. "I'll just have to make the choice *for* you!" He steps on a button concealed in the floor . . .

. . . and bamboo bars slam down out of the ceiling, surrounding you. You're trapped!

"Let me out of here!" you shout, but Nimbleton ignores you. From somewhere he's produced a huge needle and syringe, filled with foul-looking liquid.

"What shall we turn this one into?" he mutters to himself. "I think it's a good day for . . . a *hyena*."

A fat green drop of liquid falls from the needle's tip as Nimbleton approaches you . . .

THE END

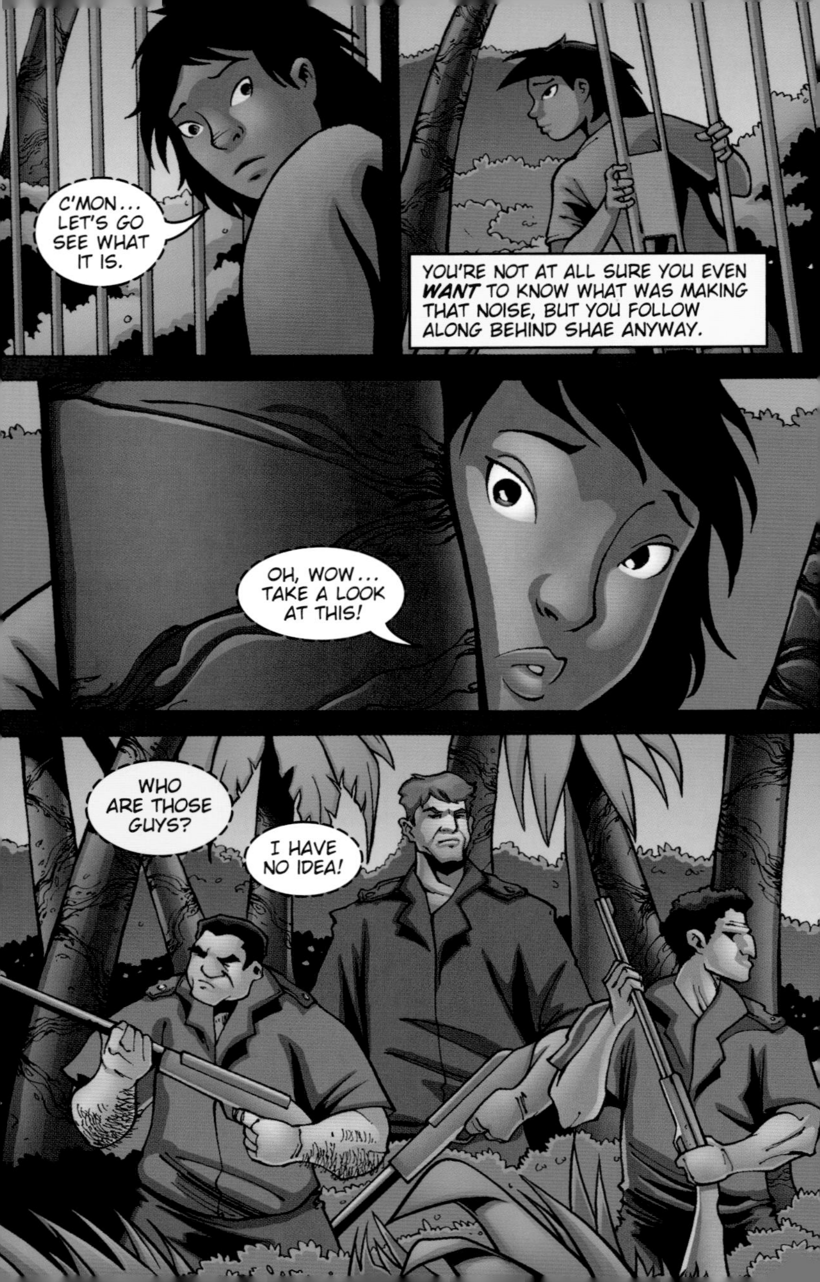
C'MON... LET'S GO SEE WHAT IT IS.
YOU'RE NOT AT ALL SURE YOU EVEN **WANT** TO KNOW WHAT WAS MAKING THAT NOISE, BUT YOU FOLLOW ALONG BEHIND SHAE ANYWAY.
OH, WOW... TAKE A LOOK AT THIS!
WHO ARE THOSE GUYS?
I HAVE NO IDEA!

"We should call out to them," Shae whispers to you. "They'll be able to help us get off the island!"

You're hesitant, though. "You've never seen these guys before, right?"

"Well . . . no."

"I haven't either. What makes you so sure they're friendly?"

Shae looks exasperated. "It's either call out to them or stay on the island. I don't really want to stay on the island. Do you?"

Before you can think of some argument that might defeat her logic, Shae moves out of the foliage and shouts, "Hey! Hey, over here!"

The men hear her and respond immediately, pushing their way toward the two of you through the undergrowth.

GO ON TO THE NEXT PAGE.

"Well, would you look at this," one of the men says, staring at you. "A couple of little lost puppies."

The biggest one, the one you think is in charge, speaks up. "We didn't realize you were children. How did you get here?"

The hairs at the back of your neck start to stand up. *We didn't realize you were children?* So they thought you and Shae were grown-ups. But that means they knew you were here! And with those guns . . . were they *hunting* you?

"What're those guns for?" you ask nervously.

The man who spoke first points his rifle right at your chest. "They're for hunting down big dogs and little puppies like you two. Henderson, put the cuffs on 'em."

The third man starts to move toward you, two pairs of handcuffs in his hands. "All these years," he says, "never bagged any children before."

They were hunting you down!
You've got to get away from them!
But you're still in the middle of the jungle.

WILL YOU . . .

. . . make a break for it and run before
Henderson can put the cuffs on you?
TURN TO PAGE 80.

. . . cooperate for now and wait for
a chance to sneak away?
TURN TO PAGE 19.

You're exhausted and hungry, and you want to get off this island more than you've ever wanted anything before. Putting on your best smile, you walk right up the path and emerge onto a small plateau.

A group of scientists are standing there, near a big tent and a boatload of high-tech equipment. All the scientists drop what they're doing and stare at you.

You don't know what to make of them. They look like something out of a sci-fi movie. One scientist stands at a long rack of test tubes and beakers, all of them filled with smoking chemicals. Another one seems to be inscribing mystic runes onto a metal plate with sulfuric acid. And yet another operates a device that's beaming a ruby red laser high into the heavens.

"Who are you?" one asks.

Another says, "How'd a little kid make it up here?"

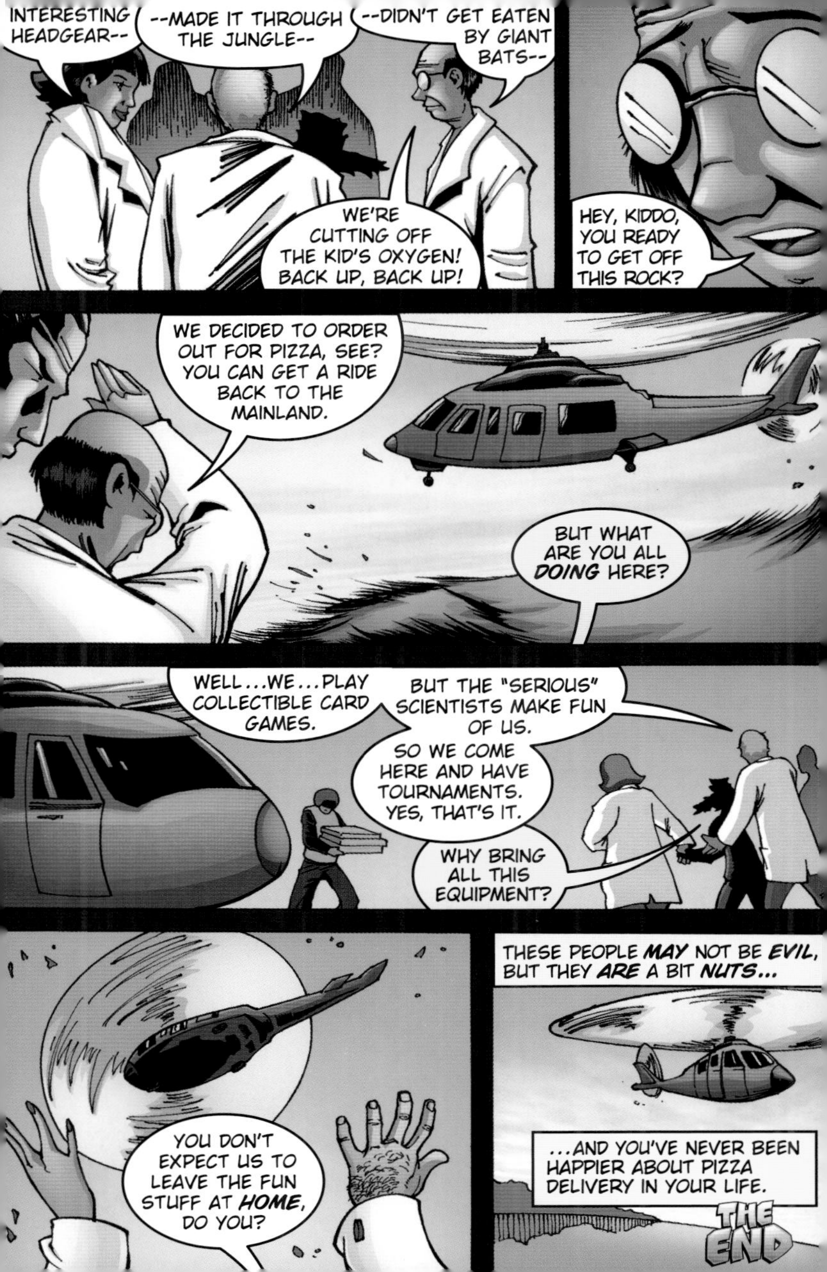
INTERESTING HEADGEAR--
--MADE IT THROUGH THE JUNGLE--
--DIDN'T GET EATEN BY GIANT BATS--
WE'RE CUTTING OFF THE KID'S OXYGEN! BACK UP, BACK UP!
HEY, KIDDO, YOU READY TO GET OFF THIS ROCK?
WE DECIDED TO ORDER OUT FOR PIZZA, SEE? YOU CAN GET A RIDE BACK TO THE MAINLAND.
BUT WHAT ARE YOU ALL DOING HERE?
WELL...WE...PLAY COLLECTIBLE CARD GAMES.
BUT THE "SERIOUS" SCIENTISTS MAKE FUN OF US.
SO WE COME HERE AND HAVE TOURNAMENTS. YES, THAT'S IT.
WHY BRING ALL THIS EQUIPMENT?
YOU DON'T EXPECT US TO LEAVE THE FUN STUFF AT HOME, DO YOU?
THESE PEOPLE MAY NOT BE EVIL, BUT THEY ARE A BIT NUTS...
...AND YOU'VE NEVER BEEN HAPPIER ABOUT PIZZA DELIVERY IN YOUR LIFE.
THE END

You and the giant sloth—which seems to have taken quite a fancy to you—follow along behind Dr. Fishcrumb as he leads you back to his laboratory. "We're working on prehistoric animals here, if you hadn't guessed."

"Like tyrannosaurs and velociraptors?" you ask.

"No, no—no dinosaurs. But we do have woolly mammoths and sabertooth tigers and obviously giant ground sloths."

"And the same storm that shipwrecked me also screwed up your equipment?"

He nods. "We had everything under control until we lost our primary *and* our secondary power generators. But once we're back inside, everything will be fine."

He leads you around a bend in the path, and there in front of you is a large concrete-and-steel building. It looks as if it would be very secure . . . if the huge metal front doors weren't hanging halfway off their hinges.

Something has broken into the place.

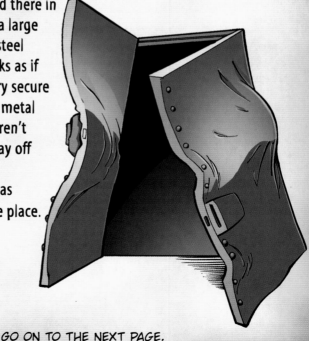

GO ON TO THE NEXT PAGE.

"This isn't good," Dr. Fishcrumb says. You can't help but agree with him.

WILL YOU . . .

. . . go into the lab, since whatever broke in might have left by now?

TURN TO PAGE 67.

. . . stay outside, where you're less likely to be trapped if something hostile is still around?

TURN TO PAGE 99.

"Yeah," you say, standing up straight. "I volunteer. Anything's better than sitting in a cage."

To your surprise, Shae stands up too. "If my friend is going, I'm going," she says. "Whatever you jerks have planned, we'll face it together."

"You don't have to do this," you whisper to her. *"Maybe I can figure out a way to help us! You might be safer down here than up there!"*

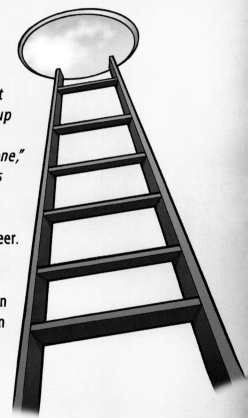

"I'm not leaving you alone," she whispers back. *"That's not what friends do."*

"Very touching," Henderson says with a sneer. "All right, fine. We'll take both of you." Speaking to another hunter, Henderson says, "Put the ladder down there. And if either of the two adults even *moves*, shoot 'em. Shoot them *both*."

You and Shae climb up out of the cell wordlessly.

ALL RIGHT,
IT'S LIKE THIS.
WE'RE GOING TO GIVE
YOU A TEN-MINUTE
HEAD START.

THEN WE'RE
COMING AFTER
YOU.

YOU'VE GOT THE
WHOLE ISLAND
TO HIDE IN.

AND
IF YOU CAN KEEP
FROM GETTING CAUGHT
TILL SUNDOWN, WE'LL NOT
ONLY LET YOU GO, WE'LL
GIVE YOU EACH A MILLION
DOLLARS.

NOT THAT I EXPECT
TO HAVE TO PAY. NO
ONE'S EVER MADE IT
TO SUNDOWN
BEFORE.

READY
TO GO?

GO ON TO THE NEXT PAGE.

Your life is at stake here!

WILL YOU . . .

. . . try to lose the hunters in the thickest part of the jungle?
TURN TO PAGE 69.

. . . run for the cave you spotted earlier?
TURN TO PAGE 86.

You remember seeing a special on TV about the African wilderness. There was a lake there that all the animals lined up around, but you don't think too many of them actually went out into the water.

But if there are crocodiles in the lake . . .

But it would be a freshwater lake, wouldn't it? Are crocodiles freshwater or salt water? Your mind blanks.

But still, if you can get to that island, you think your chances might be better than if you hang out in the jungle.

You make your way toward the lake, moving as quickly as you can. A couple of times you think you hear something . . . and once you think you might have seen some weird footprints.

But soon you're standing on the lake's shore.

THAT WASN'T A BAD SWIM AT ALL. TOO BAD YOU WERE SO WORRIED ABOUT GETTING *EATEN* THE WHOLE TIME.

MAYBE YOU CAN HOLE UP HERE FOR A WHILE... BUILD A SHELTER... CATCH SOME FISH...

AAAAAH!

AAAAAH!

SORRY! DIDN'T MEAN TO FRIGHTEN YOU!

THAT'S... THAT'S ALL RIGHT...

MY FAULT COMPLETELY!

I'VE BEEN OUT HERE SO LONG, MY MANNERS ARE ALMOST GONE!

I AM DR. GARDNER NEWCASTLE, BOTANIST! I ALONE HAVE CLASSIFIED ALL THE SPECIES ON THIS ISLAND!

TAKE THIS PREHISTORIC BEAUTY, FOR INSTANCE!

Before you have a chance to react, the flower in Dr. Newcastle's hand sprays you right in the face with a small, pungent cloud of spores. Immediately, your head starts to feel strange. Your vision begins swimming in and out of focus.

"What did you do to me?" you try to demand . . . but the words come out soft and slurred.

"The spores have a fascinating effect!" Newcastle says with glee. "They turn the average human being into a completely mindless zombie!"

Your arms and legs start to go numb. You force out a few more words: "What . . . what are you going . . . to do with me?"

"It's perfect!" he cackles. "The plant has made you into the perfect servant! You'll be sorting vegetation samples for the rest of your life! *Free labor! Hahahahaha!*"

No! This can't be happening! You can't . . . can't . . . . . . *plants . . . smell good . . . flowers pretty . . .*

THE END

You struggle against the bird's enormous talons with all your might—

—and break free! The water of the lake below you comes rushing up much faster than you expected, and you try to make your body as narrow as possible as you hit, feetfirst.

The impact almost knocks you unconscious, but you manage to fight your way over to the lake's shore.

And there, waiting for you, is a pack of the strangest creatures you've ever seen.

They're all part animal and part human, each standing on two legs—wolves, bears, tigers, and more. And they're all staring at you.

"Um . . ." You don't know what to say. They're not moving. They just stare at you. You get to your feet. "Can I help you?"

"Yes," an enormous bear-man says. "You *will* help us. Whether you like it or not."

GO ON TO THE NEXT PAGE.

You have *no* idea how to proceed here.
It's just too weird!

WILL YOU . . .

. . . hope they'll be obedient animals and
order them to let you go?
TURN TO PAGE 94.

. . . try to figure out a way to escape?
TURN TO PAGE 22.

. . . ask them why they
want your help?
TURN TO PAGE 71.

You fling yourself out of the cage at a run—

—but the tiger isn't following you. You glance over your shoulder and see Shae and a strange woman with a tranquilizer gun. They're standing over the tiger, which is slumped on the ground, unconscious!

"Dr. Margaret Pennyfeather," the woman says crisply. "Zoologist."

She explains that she's studying the ecosystem created by circus animals set loose in the jungle. "But there's more," she says. "This island is a refuge for dangerous scientists. They're called the Post-Umbral Society. Anthropologists . . . botanists . . . archaeologists . . . every one of them up to no good."

"So you're trying to stop them?" you ask.

"How can we help?" Shae asks, excited.

The doctor shakes her head. "You leave the mad scientists to me." She disappears into the trees.

"We should follow her," Shae suggests.

Before you can answer, three men in hunting gear step out from the undergrowth, holding rifles. They don't look like scientists, but they do look *dangerous*.

62 TURN TO PAGE 48.

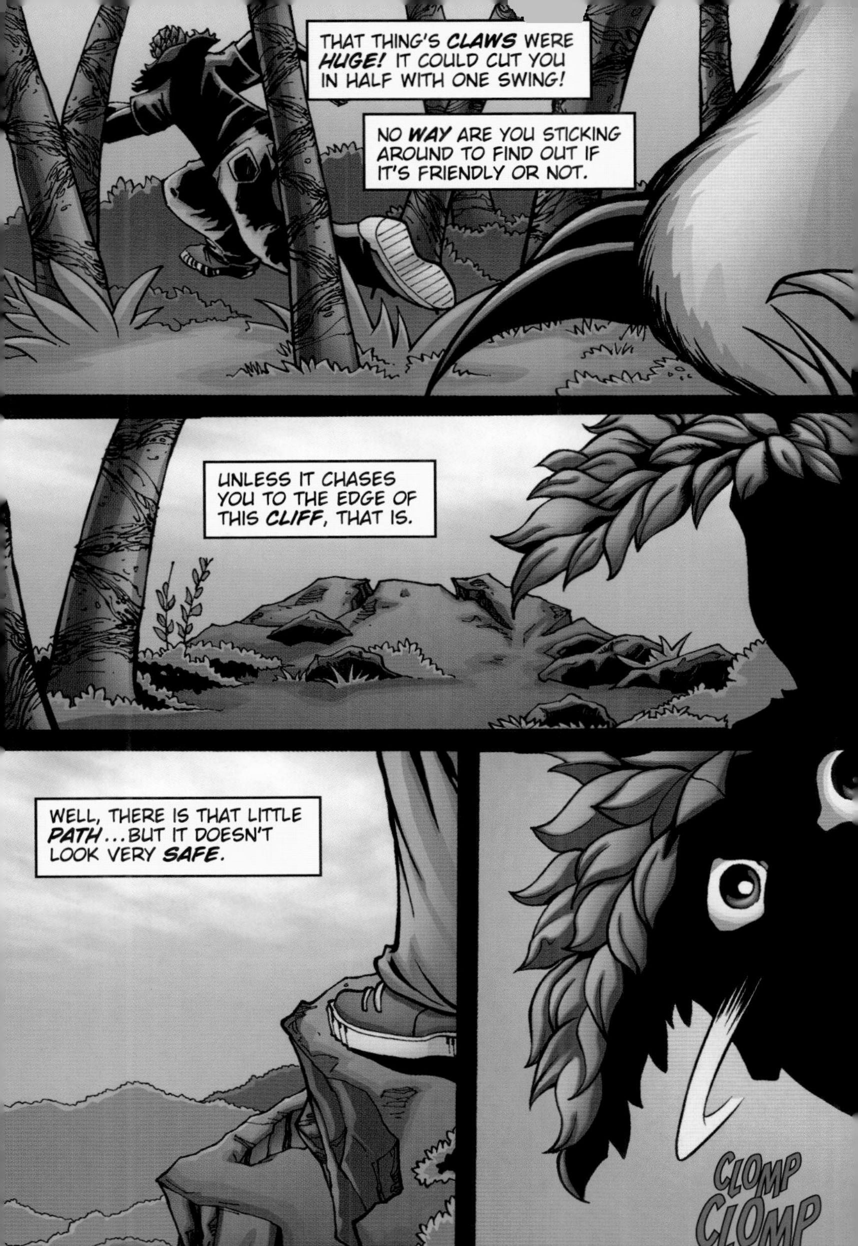
THAT THING'S CLAWS WERE HUGE! IT COULD CUT YOU IN HALF WITH ONE SWING!
NO WAY ARE YOU STICKING AROUND TO FIND OUT IF IT'S FRIENDLY OR NOT.
UNLESS IT CHASES YOU TO THE EDGE OF THIS CLIFF, THAT IS.
WELL, THERE IS THAT LITTLE PATH...BUT IT DOESN'T LOOK VERY SAFE.
CLOMP
CLOMP

[redacted] AGE.

If there's one prehistoric monster on this island, there could be lots more!

WILL YOU . . .

. . . turn around and face whatever new creature is making that noise?
TURN TO PAGE 72.

. . . decide discretion is the better part of valor and take the narrow path?
TURN TO PAGE 96.

The storm is intense. You don't think there's anywhere on this island you'll be safe. The only chance is to get into the eye of the storm, where everything's calm.

You spin around and dash back to the beach, dodging and weaving around flying debris. And yes—*there!* You think you can see an area of calm through the raging wind and rain.

Everything seems to get suddenly peaceful as you sprint onto the sand. There's no wind here. No rain. You can even see a spot of blue sky above you.

Then you hear a *whooshing* sound . . . and you see an enormous *wall of water* rushing straight at you from the ocean! Suddenly you remember: a storm like this pulls ocean water up into a deadly tidal wave called a *storm surge*.

And it's *way* too late for that knowledge to do you any good.

THE END

A frenzy of news helicopters and military aircraft descend on the island. Soon the inhabitants are rounded up into two groups: the half humans and the scientists.

If this were a bad movie, you think to yourself, *they'd get things mixed up and shoot the monsters and let the science guys go. C'mon, c'mon, don't be a bad movie!*

But you didn't have to worry. An investigation shows exactly what the scientists were up to. Every one of them goes to prison . . . and the half humans get their wish. The bear-man comes over to tell you. He's really excited!

"We're finally getting our own island!" he says, practically purring with delight. "We'll get to live in peace! And it's all thanks to you." He bows to you very formally. "You're our hero."

"Aw, shucks," you reply.

But it feels really good to be a hero.

THE END

YOU FIGURE INSIDE THE LAB HAS TO BE BETTER THAN OUTSIDE, WHERE ANYTHING COULD COME RUSHING UP ON YOU.
SO FAR SO GOOD. YOU DON'T SEE ANYTHING OUT OF THE ORDINARY YET.
ALL RIGHT, KID, WE'LL BE IN HERE. YOU EXPLORE THE LAB FOR US WHILE I...KEEP AN EYE ON DIGGER.
JUST COME AND LET US KNOW HOW THINGS WORK OUT, OKAY?
SLAM
...GREAT.
TWO THINGS STRIKE YOU AT THE SAME TIME: DOWN THE LEFT HALLWAY, SOMETHING STINKS. YOU THINK THAT'S THE WORST THING EVER...
HMM...LEFT OR RIGHT? WHICH WAY TO GO?
...UNTIL YOU HEAR SOMETHING GROWLING DOWN THE HALLWAY TO THE RIGHT.

GO ON TO THE NEXT PAGE.

You don't know what to do—there could be something bad down both hallways.

WILL YOU . . .

. . . try the stinky hallway, since whatever made it stinky might have left by now?

TURN TO PAGE 9.

. . . explore the one you heard growls from, so you can know exactly what you're facing?

TURN TO PAGE 95.

"*Go, go, go, go!*" you shout, startling the hunters for a second, as you and Shae run at top speed into the jungle. It only takes seconds for the thick vegetation to close behind you. If you didn't already know the hunters' base was only a hundred yards behind you, you'd never suspect it.

The two of you run until your lungs are burning and your feet feel like lead. Finally, you stop for a moment to rest, leaning against a huge tree. "Do you . . . think . . . we lost them?" Shae pants.

"I don't know," you answer her, just as much out of breath. "But we should keep moving."

But before you continue, you hear a sound—one you've heard before.

"I think I just heard a little electric motor," you tell Shae. "From somewhere right around here."

GO ON TO THE NEXT PAGE.

Shae's skeptical. "What kind of electric motor would be out here?"

You hear the noise again, and this time, you pinpoint it. Behind a big leaf, there's a video camera, pointed at you. "What is *that* for?" you wonder out loud.

"I'll tell you what it's for!" says a booming voice from nearby. Suddenly all the hunters come out of the jungle around you, and they're all *grinning* and *clapping!* "You've been a part of a huge experiment, to see how people act when their lives are in danger. But you spotted one of our cameras! Nicely done!"

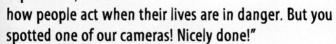

"We weren't in danger?" you ask.

"Never! These guns shoot blanks! And most of us are *actors!*"

The fake hunters take you and Shae to a boat and give you checks for huge amounts of money. "It was great working with you!" they tell you before they ship you off. "Watch for the TV special this fall! You'll be on it!"

All in all . . . there have been worse field trips.

THE END

CHILD...WE ARE PRISONERS HERE. ONCE WE WERE HUMANS. WE WERE MADE INTO THE CREATURES YOU SEE BEFORE YOU BY CRUEL SCIENTISTS.
THEY ALSO PUT *TRACKING CHIPS* IN OUR HEADS.
IF ONE OF US LEAVES THE ISLAND, THEY'LL KNOW INSTANTLY.
WE LONG TO ESCAPE, BUT THE OUTSIDE WORLD IS FAR TOO DANGEROUS FOR US.
WE NEED A COMPLETELY DESERTED ISLAND. ONE THAT ISN'T ON ANY MAP.
A PEACEFUL PLACE WHERE WE CAN LIVE OUT OUR DAYS.
AND WHAT WE NEED FROM YOU IS TO FIND SOMEONE WHO CAN HELP US.
SOMEONE WHO CAN REMOVE THE TRACKING CHIPS...AND GET US TO AN UNCHARTED ISLAND.

TURN TO PAGE 40.

You turn around, plant your feet, and try to prepare yourself for whatever you're about to see. You've watched enough monster movies for your imagination to be firing like a rocket right now. Is it a giant gorilla? A werewolf? A big guy with a hockey mask and a chain saw?

But instead of any of those things, the thick vegetation parts . . . and a normal-looking guy in a white lab coat walks out of the jungle. He has a notepad in one hand and some sort of high-tech device in the other, and he's not paying any attention to you at all.

What kind of scientist wanders around a weird tropical island? He doesn't have any sort of protective gear on that you can see. He's just an ordinary guy.

GO ON TO THE NEXT PAGE.

The scientist looks harmless enough. But is something so out of place a sign of trouble?

WILL YOU . . .

. . . try to get the scientist's attention?
TURN TO PAGE 85.

. . . find a place to hide so he doesn't see you?
TURN TO PAGE 103.

DANGEROUS OR NOT, YOU'VE GOT TO FIND OUT WHAT THAT LIGHT WAS. LIGHT EQUALS CIVILIZATION, AND CIVILIZATION EQUALS A WAY HOME.
BUT ONCE YOU SEE WHERE THE LIGHT WAS COMING FROM...
...YOU'RE NOT SURE WHETHER IT MEANS CIVILIZATION OR NOT.
WHAT DO YOU SAY TO A STRANGE GIRL IN THE MIDDLE OF A JUNGLE?
UM... HI?
AAH!

The girl stares at you with huge, wide eyes, and you realize you must look pretty strange, with your bedraggled clothing and your big leaf-hat. Still, it only takes her a couple of seconds before she asks, "Would you like to come inside? There's room enough for you."

You thank her and step into the cage. She immediately starts pulling heavy, handwoven bamboo-and-leaf covers over the sides, sealing the cage pretty tightly. "This won't protect us if the storm gets very bad," she says, "but it'll keep out most of the rain and wind if the weather behaves."

"Thanks!" You notice how skillfully the covers are put together. "Did you make these things yourself?"

"I sure did," she tells you. "My name's Shae. It's nice to meet you."

You shake Shae's hand, impressed. "How long have you been here?"

She gestures at the covers. "Long enough to make all of these."

GO ON TO THE NEXT PAGE.

The rain seems to be slowing down. You sit back on your haunches and watch Shae for a few moments. She seems very calm and confident. "How did you get here?" you ask her.

"Helicopter crash," she says simply.

You glance around the cage. "I thought you must have been part of the circus or something."

She turns serious eyes on you. "No. This cage was here when I got here. I'm afraid boats and aircraft have been crashing on this island for a *long* time."

Suddenly, from outside, you hear the sound of something big moving through the jungle, very close by. *"What is that?"* you ask Shae in a whisper.

She narrows her eyes. "Maybe something bad. Maybe something good," she says. "I've glimpsed something moving in the jungle before, but I could never tell what it was."

GO ON TO THE NEXT PAGE.

"What do *you* think we should do?" Shae asks.
That's an excellent question.

WILL YOU . . .

. . . stay put and see if the
thing outside goes away?
TURN TO PAGE 83.

. . . leave the cage and investigate?
TURN TO PAGE 46.

I'M JUST A **KID!** I DON'T KNOW HOW TO DO **ANY** OF THIS STUFF YOU'RE ASKING ME TO DO!
I'M SORRY. I JUST CAN'T HELP YOU.
YOU'RE POSITIVE, THEN? YOU CANNOT DO WHAT WE ASK?
ALL RIGHT. WE UNDERSTAND. IT IS A GREAT DEAL TO ASK OF SOMEONE.
I'M SORRY. I JUST NEED TO GET HOME.
IF YOU GO TO THE OTHER SIDE OF THE ISLAND, THROUGH THE JUNGLE, THERE IS A SMALL RAFT ON THE SHORE.
IT SHOULD BE ENOUGH TO GET YOU TO THE MAINLAND.
JUST BE CAREFUL OF THE HUMANS... THE **SCIENTISTS**. THEY ARE DANGEROUS.

GO ON TO THE NEXT PAGE.

You head through the jungle until you get to the other side of the island. There, sure enough, is a little raft—it's just some bamboo lashed together, but it should be enough to get you off this island.

You feel a little guilty for refusing to help them, but hey . . . what are you going to do? If the choice is between helping them and saving your own skin, well, there *is* no choice, is there?

Suddenly you feel a sharp sting on the back of your neck. You reach back . . . and pull out a tranquilizer dart! Your knees hit the sand before you even realize you're going to fall. You try to stay upright, as a group of scientists comes and stands around you.

"Look at this," one says. "I think we should turn the child into a kangaroo rat."

The others agree.

And everything goes black.

THE END

"Run!" you scream, and Shae must've been thinking the exact same thing, because the two of you dart away from the hunters simultaneously. Shae's right by your side as you slip into the undergrowth, moving as fast as you can, trying to put as much distance as possible between yourselves and the men with the guns.

"Where are we going?" Shae gasps, breathless, just loud enough for you to hear.

"I don't know!" How could she expect you to know where to go? She's been here a lot longer than you have!

But then it becomes a moot point, at least for Shae. As you watch, a small, brightly feathered dart hits the side of her neck and she tumbles face-first to the jungle floor. She's been tranquilized.

You don't have time to try to help her. The hunters are coming.

YOU'VE GOT TO KEEP MOVING! YOU'RE SURE THEY'LL TRANQUILIZE YOU TOO IF THEY GET A CLEAR SHOT.
COME BACK HERE, LITTLE PUPPY PUPPY PUPPY!
THAT LOOKS LIKE A CLEARING UP AHEAD!
MAYBE YOU CAN USE THAT TO PUT ON AN EXTRA BURST OF SPEED.
EXCEPT IT WASN'T A CLEARING AT ALL. YOU'VE JUST RUN RIGHT OVER THE EDGE OF A CLIFF.
YOUR LAST THOUGHT, AS THE GROUND RUSHES UP:
WORST
FIELD TRIP
EVER.
THE

That night the half humans build a bonfire in the middle of the scientists' base. They break open the freezer and cook food over the fire on long sticks.

You talk to the huge bear-man. "What are you going to do with all these scientists?"

He seems thoughtful. "Well, we can't kill them. I suppose we'll take them out into the ocean and put them in a lifeboat with some food. Let them find their way from there."

"Sounds like a plan." You pause. "What are you and the rest of your people going to do?"

The bear-man shrugs. "Whatever we want to, I guess. Tell you what. You're a huge hero to us now. How about we relax and enjoy the festivities tonight, and we'll worry about getting you home tomorrow?"

You give him your biggest grin. "I like the sound of that."

THE END

YOU AND SHAE SIT AS QUIETLY AS YOU CAN. YOU DON'T KNOW WHAT IS OUTSIDE...
...BUT WHATEVER IT IS...
...IT'S *BIG*.
RROOOOAAR
GRRNNKK
WE CAN'T STAY HERE!

GO ON TO THE NEXT PAGE.

There's no choice now. You have to get out of that cage! But once you get the door open,

WILL YOU . . .

. . . dash back to the beach? Cats don't like water, right?
TURN TO PAGE 93.

. . . run farther into the jungle and try to lose it in the dense underbrush?
TURN TO PAGE 62.

"H-h-hello," you stammer anxiously.

The scientist looks up, astonished. "Who are you?" he asks. "How'd you get here?"

You explain about the shipwreck and tell him about the giant sloth you saw. "Oh!" he says. "That's just my robot! I built him for a museum exhibit. Come with me, I'll introduce you properly. Plus, I bet you'd like a grilled cheese sandwich, huh?"

The scientist's name is Dr. Feezil McCrockley. He takes you back to his secluded research lab, where you see the giant robot sloth, along with giant robot trilobites, Rhamphorhynchuses, and frogs.

"You made giant robot *frogs*?" you ask

Dr. McCrockley shrugs. "I like frogs."

He does indeed give you a grilled cheese sandwich— quite possibly the best one you've ever tasted—and then radios the mainland.

You wave good-bye as you leave on the helicopter. You almost wish you could stay longer.

Almost.

THE END

"They'll never find us in that cave, I bet!" you tell Shae breathlessly as the two of you make a mad dash for it. "It'll be too dark!"

Shae doesn't seem convinced. "Uh . . . won't they have flashlights?"

But you hear the hunters shouting behind you and know you don't have time to second-guess yourself. You and Shae make it to the cave and run inside, grateful for the darkness that swallows you up.

Minutes pass. Everything stays quiet. No hunters . . . no nothing.

"I think they gave up," you tell Shae. "I don't think they're coming in here."

You can feel Shae shivering in the dark. "Maybe that's because they know better."

"Come on!" you scoff. "What could possibly scare *those* guys?"

In response, a deep voice from the darkness behind you says, "I believe I know the answer to that question." A flashlight clicks on, lighting a craggy, bearded face.

86

GO ON TO THE NEXT PAGE.

I KNOW VANDALS WHEN I SEE THEM!
YOU WANT TO DESTROY MY CAVE PAINTINGS!
I'LL MAKE SURE YOU NEVER DESTROY ANYTHING AGAIN!
WHO THE--
DR. PAVEL OLIVERA, WE MEET AT LAST.
DR. MARGARET PENNYFEATHER, ZOOLOGIST AND ADVENTURER, AT YOUR SERVICE.
PENNYFEATHER! HOW DID YOU FIND ME?
IT'S NOT HARD TO LOCATE A RENEGADE ARCHAEOLOGIST WITH A LONG RECORD OF KIDNAPPING AND MURDER.
WHATEVER MYSTICAL, MIND-CONTROLLING ANCIENT SECRET YOU'RE TRYING TO UNEARTH, YOU CAN JUST FORGET IT.
YOU'LL NEVER TAKE ME IN!

The tall, slender woman springs past you and Shae. She knocks Olivera's legs out from under him, flips him on his stomach, and soon has him hog-tied.

"That was awesome!" Shae exclaims.

"All in a day's work bringing down the Post-Umbral Society," she says. "Those evil scientists are intent on banding together to control the world," she tells you. "Which is why it's much too dangerous for the two of you to stay on this island."

"What, you think I *want* to stay here?" You laugh. "If you can get me away from this island, the sooner, the better!"

Shae agrees with you, so Dr. Pennyfeather puts you both on a helicopter within the hour.

You're sure it's exciting, battling mad scientists. But you'd much rather see it on the evening news than live it.

THE END

OUR PLAN IS PROCEEDING BRILLIANTLY! SOON THE POST-UMBRAL SOCIETY WILL UNLEASH OUR GENETICALLY ALTERED GIANT VAMPIRE BATS UPON THE WORLD.
THEN ALL PLANET EARTH WILL BEG US TO HELP THEM. AND WE SHALL... FOR A PRICE.
HEY, IS SOMEBODY OVER THERE?
THIS IS SOME SORT OF DEN OF EVIL MAD SCIENTISTS! YOU'VE GOT TO WARN SOMEONE!
Skreeeeee
HEY!
GIANT BAT?
HEEEEEEEEEEEEYYYYYYYY!!
TOO BAD... NOW YOU WON'T BE WARNING ANYONE OF ANYTHING...!
THE END

IMMEDIATELY YOU KNOW THIS WAS THE RIGHT DECISION.
THE NOISE OF THE STORM GROWS QUIETER THE FARTHER INTO THE CAVE YOU GO.
BUT WAIT A MINUTE! THIS IS LIKE NO CAVE YOU'VE EVER HEARD OF BEFORE!
SOMEONE HAS GONE TO A HUGE AMOUNT OF EFFORT TO BUILD THIS.
IT'S EITHER EXPLORE OR GO BACK OUT INTO THE STORM...BUT THIS PLACE FEELS CREEPY.
H-HELLO? CAN YOU HELP ME?
WHAT HAVE WE HERE, THEN?
A WEE LITTLE RABBIT, BOUNDING IN FROM THE NASTY WEATHER?
PLEASED TO MEET YOU, MY FRIEND! I'M DR. KRAKOW. DR. OLIVIA KRAKOW.

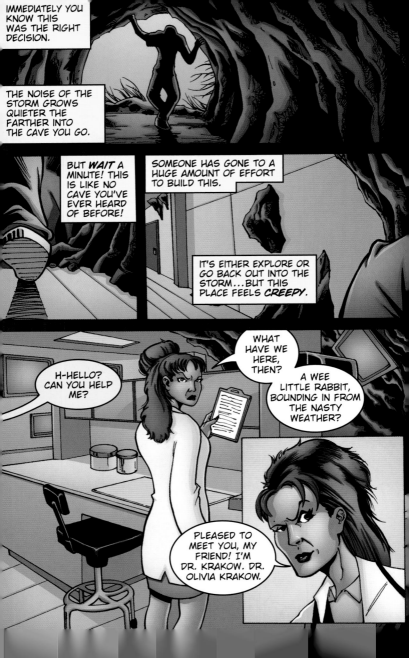

"I'm sure you have the best of intentions," you tell Dr. Fishcrumb, "but I'm going to take a look around on my own."

"Don't be an idiot," he snaps. "You're in way over your head."

"Exactly! That's why I want to look around!" You leave Dr. Fishcrumb and Digger behind and start heading toward higher ground.

Soon you make it to a rock outcropping, about halfway up a craggy, mountainous slope. You're exhausted by the time you get there, but as soon as you turn around, you know the effort was worth it.

Half of the island spreads out below you. Most of it is dense jungle . . . but there, a couple of miles away, is a lake. And in the middle of the lake, you see a nice, green, peaceful-looking island. The island is dotted with perfect flowers and perfectly spaced trees.

GO ON TO THE NEXT PAGE.

TWISTED JOURNEYS®

The little island might be a good refuge . . .
but there's more to this place
that you haven't seen yet.

WILL YOU . . .

. . . try to make it to the little island?
TURN TO PAGE 57.

. . . keep going higher, so you can see the other
side of this place when you get to the top?
TURN TO PAGE 100.

You take a deep breath and shove the door open. You and Shae are out of the cage in a flash.

"Come on!" you shout, heading back toward the beach. "Cats don't like to get wet! We'll jump in the ocean and be safe!"

"Okay!" Shae follows you. You hear the tiger roar again, very close by.

The wind and rain are monstrous, but they don't stop you. You power through the jungle to the beach, sprint across the sand, and fling yourselves into the ocean.

And the tiger comes in right behind you. Not only that, but it's a strong swimmer—stronger than you are.

"I thought you said tigers don't like to get wet?" Shae screams.

You realize your mistake: *Lions* don't like to get wet. Tigers swim all the time.

And that's the last thought you have before the tiger catches you.

THE END

YOU DON'T KNOW IF THIS IS GOING TO WORK OR NOT... BUT IT WORKS OKAY WITH THE NEIGHBORHOOD DOGS.

BAD! BAD BEAR! THAT WAS *VERY* RUDE! YOU DON'T *FORCE* PEOPLE TO HELP YOU.

IS THAT KID... *SCOLDING* US?

I BELIEVE SO.

WE DON'T *LIKE* TO BE SCOLDED.

You move silently down the hallway, your footsteps making not even a whisper against the cold tile floor. You hear the low, rumbling growl again, coming from up ahead. There are three doors ahead of you: one straight in front and one each on your right and left. All three stand open, only darkness visible in the doorways, and you can't tell from which one the growl came.

As soon as I know what it is, I'll get out of here, you tell yourself. You can't stand not knowing! What if it's something harmless, like Digger?

Then you hear another growl . . . from behind you.

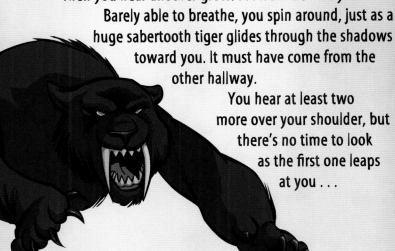

Barely able to breathe, you spin around, just as a huge sabertooth tiger glides through the shadows toward you. It must have come from the other hallway.

You hear at least two more over your shoulder, but there's no time to look as the first one leaps at you . . .

THE END

You start edging down the narrow cliff path. You have to press your body to the rock to keep from falling off.

You remember reading somewhere that rock climbing is not about how strong you are. It's how well you balance your center of gravity, to pull yourself up an almost sheer rock face.

Well, you're descending, not climbing, but you already know this is just as much about balance. The ledge gets narrower and narrower, until it's no wider than the average chalkboard eraser.

This is nuts! you say to yourself. *I've got to go back up!*

You risk a glance down along the ledge and see a much wider rocky shelf below.

And the strip of rock you're standing on begins to crumble.

You'll never make it back up to the top. Your only hope is to get to the wide, rocky shelf.

WILL YOU . . .

. . . rush along the ledge as fast as you can before it crumbles away?
TURN TO PAGE 18.

. . . be extra careful and take your time, so you don't make the ledge crumble any faster?
TURN TO PAGE 36.

THE MOST IMPORTANT THING RIGHT NOW IS TO GET A SENSE OF EXACTLY WHAT YOU'RE DEALING WITH.

AND IT LOOKS AS THOUGH YOU'RE DEALING WITH A WHOLE LOT OF JUNGLE.

YOU'RE STARTING TO THINK YOU MIGHT AS WELL JUST HEAD BACK TO THE BEACH...

...WHEN YOUR DAY SUDDENLY GETS A WHOLE LOT WORSE.

LET ME GO!

LET ME GO!

TURN TO PAGE 8.

"There's no way I'm going in there," you tell Dr. Fishcrumb.

"Don't be ridiculous," he grumbles at you. "There's a safe room. It's secure. You'll be fine."

"Oh yeah?" You gesture at the ruined metal doors at the building's entrance. "Were those doors supposed to be 'safe' too? Forget it. I'm staying right here."

Dr. Fishcrumb's frown turns into a full-blown scowl. "We're in danger out here right now. You don't realize what you're doing."

You take a breath to reply, but before you can get the first word out, the ground starts to tremble. An awful, deafening noise thunders all around you . . .

. . . and a whole section of trees gets flattened as an entire herd of woolly mammoths come stampeding into the clearing!

Neither you nor the doctor can react in time, and the world disappears under colossal, trampling feet. The last thing you hear is Dr. Fishcrumb's voice: "I told you soooo!"

THE END

You keep climbing. It'd be best to know all you can about where you are, right? What if there turned out to be a trading post or a camp or even a town on the other side of this rise?

As you climb, you try to remember everything you've ever learned about surviving in the wilderness. You know you can make a fire by rubbing two sticks together, or at least, you think you can do that. You know that mushrooms with a little ring around the stalk are always poisonous, and anyway, you should *never* eat any mushrooms you find, unless you *really* know how to identify them. That's pretty crucial to survival in the wild. You know the sun comes up in the east and sets in the west.

You're distracted by a sound from somewhere farther ahead, a sound that you can't quite place. It's very high pitched, sort of like . . . squeaking? Squealing?

What *is* that?

GO ON TO THE NEXT PAGE.

YOU FEEL AS THOUGH YOU'RE MAKING PRETTY GOOD PROGRESS...UNTIL YOU RUN UP AGAINST A SHEER ROCK WALL.
YOU THINK YOU COULD PROBABLY CLIMB IT. AND IF YOU WANT TO GET TO THE TOP, THAT'S DEFINITELY THE MOST DIRECT ROUTE.
ON THE OTHER HAND, THERE'S PROBABLY ANOTHER WAY AROUND. AND CLIMBING IS ***REALLY*** HARD!
SQUEAK SQUEAK

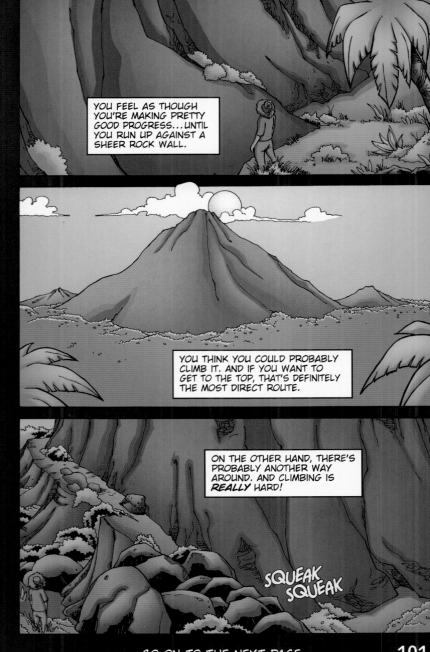

GO ON TO THE NEXT PAGE.

You don't want to waste any
time, but you also want to be as
safe as you can be.

WILL YOU . . .

. . . play it cautious and look for
a longer way around?
TURN TO PAGE 25.

. . . try to save time and climb
straight up the rock face?
TURN TO PAGE 37.

You hop down onto the narrow ledge and crouch, doing your best to hide and be still . . .

. . . and it works! The scientist doesn't notice you at all. He bumbles his way back into the jungle. You heave a sigh of relief and cast a quick glance down the path . . .

. . . and then you almost jump out of your skin in surprise. Crouched on the path, not ten feet below you, is someone dressed in black from head to foot, including a completely face-covering black mask. Infrared-vision goggles cover the person's eyes, but it's obvious he—or she—is watching you.

The black-clad stranger stands up, and you realize it's someone about your age! You can't tell if it's a boy or a girl, though.

"Hello," the stranger says. "You can call me Code name: Mongoose. What do I call you?"

SO WHO ARE YOU? WHY ARE YOU DRESSED LIKE THAT?
LET'S JUST SAY I WORK FOR A SECRET ORGANIZATION THAT'S TAKEN A KEEN INTEREST IN THINGS HAPPENING ON THIS ISLAND.
CLICK WHIRRR
FLIP FLIP CLICK
THIS IS NOT A PLACE FOR CIVILIANS. WOULD YOU LIKE TO GO BACK TO THE MAINLAND?
IS THAT A JET PACK? I DON'T KNOW HOW TO FLY ONE OF THOSE!
I'LL SET THE AUTOPILOT.
I MIGHT HAVE TO GET A LITTLE UNRULY HERE, AND I DON'T WANT YOU TO GET CAUGHT IN ANY CROSS FIRE.
WHEN A SECRET AGENT OFFERS YOU A CHANCE TO FLY HOME USING A JET PACK...
...HOW CAN YOU SAY NO?
THE END

The creatures are peaceful now . . . but for how long?
You break free of them and run across the sand to the
group of scientists.

"Thank goodness you found
me!" you say to the closest of the
scientists, a tall, blond-haired man.

"Yeah," he says, in a voice
rougher than you'd
expect to hear from a
man of science. "That
could've been really
bad." Then he pulls a
small device from
his coat pocket
and fires a needle
right into your
neck.

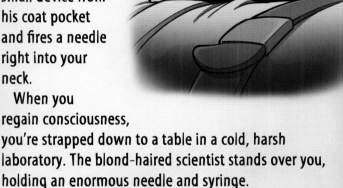

When you
regain consciousness,
you're strapped down to a table in a cold, harsh
laboratory. The blond-haired scientist stands over you,
holding an enormous needle and syringe.

"Now hold still," he says. "We're about to turn you into
a half lemur."

You start to scream, but as soon as you feel the sting
of the shot, the world turns gray and hazy and fades
away . . .

THE END

Slowly, carefully, you step forward and hold out one hand. The sloth squints at you with its beady little eyes and moves closer. It's *really* slow, but it's so huge that the ground vibrates every time it puts down one of its enormous, clawed front feet.

"N-n-n-nice sloth," you say quietly. "Hi there. I'm not going to hurt you." It occurs to you how ridiculous that sounds. Of *course* you're not going to hurt it. You couldn't if you wanted to. But still. "Are you a good sloth? Are you a good, nice, very friendly sloth?"

The sloth leans its head forward . . . and licks your hand! It even pushes its muzzle into your hand so you can pet it. You start stroking its nose and scratching behind its ears. It *is* friendly!

Suddenly a man's voice calls out from the jungle. "Digger! Digger, where'd you go?"

The sloth turns toward the voice.

GO ON TO THE NEXT PAGE.

THERE YOU ARE!

I LOSE SIGHT OF YOU FOR TWO SECONDS, YOU BIG LUMMOX, AND YOU BRING BACK A *KID*?

SORRY, DIGGER, YOU CAN'T KEEP IT. IT DOESN'T LOOK HOUSEBROKEN.

EVEN IF THAT STORM HADN'T KNOCKED OUT OUR SECURITY SYSTEM, I WOULDN'T HAVE THE TIME TO ANSWER QUESTIONS.

ESPECIALLY WHEN I'VE LOST TRACK OF SOME SPECIMENS.

WHO ARE YOU? WHAT IS THIS PLACE?

WAIT... "SPECIMENS"?

NAME'S KENSINGTON FISHCRUMB. YOU CAN CALL ME *DOCTOR* FISHCRUMB...DID YOU HEAR THAT SOUND?

UHH... WHAT SOUND?

THE SOUND OF US STANDING AROUND *WASTING TIME* WHILE FEROCIOUS PREDATORS ROAM THE JUNGLE.

I DON'T KNOW WHAT YOUR PLANS ARE, KID, BUT THE SLOTH AND I ARE HEADING SOMEWHERE MORE *SECURE*.

GO ON TO THE NEXT PAGE.

You don't know whether to be alarmed or not,
but you've got to do *something*.

WILL YOU . . .

. . . go with Dr. Fishcrumb and Digger?
TURN TO PAGE 52.

. . . decide Dr. Fishcrumb is too weird and rude
and strike out on your own?
TURN TO PAGE 91.

. . . climb a nearby tall tree to get a
better lay of the land?
TURN TO PAGE 98.

Before you even realize what's happening, two of the half humans grab you and bind your wrists and ankles with long lengths of jungle vine. Then the whole pack retreats into the jungle, carrying you along with them as if you were a sack of potatoes.

Soon the bizarre group enters a clearing deep within the wilderness, and you can see the yawning mouth of a huge cave ahead. The group immediately enters the cave . . .

. . . and inside you see a cage built of bamboo and animal bones. There's a man in the cage—a human!

The half humans throw you inside without any further conversation. The man lifts his head and looks at you with weary eyes.

"What are you in here for?" you ask him.

Blandly he tells you, "I disrespected the Pack out there."

Your shoulders slump. "Great."

GO ON TO THE NEXT PAGE.

"It's time for you to meet justice," the bear-man says. You see two oddly shaped gourds in his hand. "We have stolen this elixir from Dr. Nimbleton, the thrice-cursed scientist who did this to us."

"O-o-okay," you stammer. "What does that 'elixir' do, exactly?"

"It makes you understand," he replies as he opens the cage. "You shall drink it now."

He's way too strong to resist. The bear-man pours the liquid down your throat, and your hands start to feel incredibly weird. In fact, your whole *body* feels weird . . . as if you were . . . *transforming!*

In less than ten minutes, it's complete: You're now half human and half tree sloth.

They leave you hanging upside down in a tree.

At least you're alive . . . though it isn't really much of a life.

THE END

NATURALLY YOU'LL BE WANTING THE GRAND TOUR OF THE FACILITIES.
I, UH, JUST WANT TO USE THE PHONE...
OF COURSE I'LL SHOW YOU MY LIFE'S WORK.
YOU SEE, THE OTHER MEMBERS OF THE POST-UMBRAL SOCIETY AND I HAVE BEEN ATTEMPTING TO CONTROL THE WEATHER. AND WE'VE FINALLY DONE IT!
STAND ON THIS RED CIRCLE.
THE STORM THAT BROUGHT YOU HERE WAS ONE OF OURS.
YOU CAUSED THAT STORM? MY CLASSMATES AND I COULD HAVE BEEN KILLED! YOU CAN'T JUST ZAP PEOPLE LIKE THAT!
OH, NO?
ZAP!
HAHAHAHA! SOON I SHALL UNLEASH THE WRATH OF MY LIGHTNING GENERATOR UPON THE WORLD!
WELL. DR. KRAKOW IS OBVIOUSLY NUTS.
NOT THAT THAT MATTERS TO YOU ANYMORE.
THE END

WHICH TWISTED JOURNEYS® WILL YOU TRY NEXT?